EMORY'S
Mate

Lynn Howard

Emory's Mate
Lynn Howard
@2019
Published by Twisted Heart Press, LLC

Chapter One

Eli paced the property line butting up against the Big River Pack territory. No. It wasn't Eli pacing. It was his fucking lion. Every night he ended up here, watching, guarding, protecting his mate, even if she wanted nothing to do with him. His lion had chosen and had become obsessed. No matter how hard Eli tried, even taking enough sleeping pills to knock out a horse, his lion always ended up here.

Eli was fucking exhausted.

The sun would be up soon and the Pack would be climbing from their beds and starting their day. And Emory would take a quick shower, search the woods as if she sensed him there, then head into town for work. It had been the same ritual for the past three weeks.

Lying down on the dry leaves and hard, drought-dried ground, he waited for the squeak of her pipes. Both sides of Eli fantasized about how she looked when she stepped under that spray of hot water; how she'd look with the moisture rolling down her naked body.

His lion might have been the one dragging him out here every night, but it was Eli who was left jerking off in his shower every day after. Surely, that much masturbating wasn't good for anyone.

Eli's lion lifted his head and his ears quirked forward; she was up. Emory was out of bed and moving around her little place. He waited for the sound of her shower but was surprised when her steps moved closer to the door and it swung open. She stood on her porch in the hazy gray light of dawn and searched the trees, her eyes squinted. Did she know he was out there? Was that why her eyes immediately hit the tree line every single morning? Was she searching for him?

Eli hurried to his feet when Emory stepped from her porch and stomped right in his direction. Her eyes were still wandering the area like she hadn't spotted him, but she definitely knew he was in the shadows.

Once Emory was far enough from the row of houses, she lifted her head and frowned. "I know you're there, Eli. Come out."

With a huff, he Shifted back into his human form and slowly made his way into the light so she could see him. Her Shifter abilities allowed her to see and hear far more than any human, but her senses weren't nearly as acute as his lion's.

Emory stopped walking and stood stock still, her eyes wide and darting from his face to his junk then back again. "Could you at least cover your dick?" she asked, relaxing her face and placing a scowl firmly in place.

But Eli hadn't missed it; there'd been obvious appreciation and even a little lust in her eyes when he'd stepped into view naked. She wouldn't admit it, but Emory liked what she'd seen.

Cupping himself, Eli kept moving until he was a few feet away from her.

"What are you doing here, Eli?" she asked, keeping her head raised and crossing her arms under her breasts. It took everything he had not to dip his eyes to her perfectly framed tits.

"I don't know," he said.

"Bullshit. I know you've been coming around the last couple weeks."

"Three," he said, his eyes dropping to the ground before raising back to her face.

"What?"

"Three weeks."

It had been three weeks since he'd lost complete control over his animal. He'd been able to stay away after he'd marked her to protect her during a battle against his Pride and a rival Pack to Big River, but the longer he went without seeing her, without knowing she was safe, the more unsteady he was becoming. The only way to keep his lion from attacking his own Pride members was by stalking the beautiful woman glaring at him.

"Why? Why are you here? You promised you'd leave me alone." Her arms dropped to her sides and she looked defeated for a brief second.

"I tried," he admitted, his eyes dropping to the ground at her feet again. He had a hard time staring into her beautiful turquoise eyes.

She was so tiny, standing over a foot shorter than his six-foot-two. And she was petite. Oh, there was muscle definition in her arms and legs. He could see that clearly with the shorts and tank top she was wearing. But even though she was a Shifter and strong, his lion saw her as fragile.

"Try harder," she said, narrowing her eyes at him. She turned on her heel to walk away.

"Wait," he said, raising his arm to touch her while taking a step in her direction.

When she whirled on him, so much fire in her eyes, he let his arm drop away from her quickly.

"For what, Eli? You promised me you'd leave me alone. You said this," she said, pointing a finger at the marks on the back of her neck, "meant nothing. Or was that one big fucking lie?"

"No...yes. I don't know," he said, dragging a hand down his face then pushing it through his hair.

"Which is it, Eli?"

He propped both hands on his hips, then immediately went back to cupping his junk when her eyes dropped between his legs then darted back up to his face. "It's not me."

She cocked her head to the side with a dark brow raised.

"Seriously. I tried. I really did. It's my lion. He was going insane. I thought if I allowed him to check on you, just let him see you were okay, he'd calm down."

"But he didn't," she said rather than asked.

"He didn't," he agreed. "I've tried everything. I even tried drugs."

Her brows dropped low. "Great. My mate is a drug addict?"

His lips popped open and his face went slack when she called him her mate. She'd admitted it, said it out loud, but instead of punching his fist into the air, he tried to gloss over that little statement. Especially since she looked like she wanted to shove her tiny foot in her mouth.

"No. I'm not a drug addict, Emory. I was taking sleeping pills. I thought it worked until I started waking up with leaves in my bed. And then they no longer worked on me, either. He kept fighting my Pride."

"Good," she muttered under her breath. He knew Emory hated his Pride for what they'd done to her Pack, for what they'd done to the Second's mate, Callie, but they weren't the same Pride anymore. Eli had been shoved into the Alpha position, and he'd immediately made changes to the way they lived their lives. Namely, he'd declared all lionesses free to go if they chose. There were no longer any forced pairings permitted within Tammen Pride territory.

"Not good, Emory. I'm the Alpha as long as I can maintain some semblance of power and control. If the others get a whiff of how unstable my fucking lion is, they'll challenge me and possibly win. And then we'll have another Rhett situation on our hands."

Emory sucked her bottom lip into her mouth and chewed on it, drawing Eli's attention there. Her lips were so pretty, so naturally pink and full. He'd bet they were soft, too. Both sides of him wanted to drag her against his naked body and taste her, dip his tongue into her mouth, and see how many little sounds he could pull from her.

"Did the lionesses leave?" she asked, yanking him out of his fantasies about how she'd taste.

"Not all of them," he said.

"Why not?"

He lifted one shoulder, careful to keep himself tucked in the palm of his hand. "Most of them have nowhere else to go, Emory. They were sold off or handed to Rhett by their own families. Pretty sure they wouldn't be welcomed back. Then again, would you want to return to a family where your only value was how much you were worth to another Pride?"

Her eyes moved to the left and she went back to worrying her bottom lip. So many emotions flitted over her face, but they were gone before he could name any of them. What was she thinking about? Was she sad for the lionesses who were stuck in a Pride they never wanted? Was she happy he was changing the rules of his Pride?

Or was she thinking about something that had nothing to do with him or his Pride?

"Look," she said after a few minutes of silence. "Just try to keep your lion under wraps, okay? I'm fine. I'm safe. I have my own Pack to look after me. And I really don't think Gray or Micah, or, hell, any of my family would be too happy about having a lion in our territory with the baby."

Nova and Gray's baby. She'd given birth just before Rhett had attacked. And Eli knew as a fact that hadn't been by accident. Rhett had wanted the Pack at their most vulnerable. He'd wanted some kind of bargaining chip to get Callie back as a breeder. What better way than to threaten a newborn?

"I'll do my best. But I can't make any promises."

"Yeah, you already did that and didn't keep them," she said, throwing her hand in the air as she turned again to walk away.

"What if…" He trailed off, unsure if what he was about to suggest was his greatest idea or dumbest.

She stopped walking but didn't turn back to look at him. "What if what, Eli?"

He took a step in her direction, but stayed far enough back to keep her from feeling like he was a threat.

"What if we hung out?"

She turned a little and looked at him over her shoulder "What?" she asked, a disbelieving look all over her stunning face.

"We can meet up somewhere; you don't even have to ride with me. Just…hang out at Moe's or something. Or maybe you could try texting me every once in a while, just to let me know you're okay. Maybe that'll settle my animal."

She was back to worrying her bottom lip. He wanted to reach up and smooth the line between her brows and pull her lip from her teeth. He wanted to press his lips to hers. But, instead, he stood there, his hand holding his dick and balls, and waited for her answer.

"Just hang out," she said, finally turning fully to look at him. "No strings."

"No strings. Just let my lion know you're safe. I don't know if it'll work, but it's worth a try."

What he really wanted to tell her was he wanted her just as much as his lion, but he had a little more willpower than that. He wanted her in his life, in his arms, in his house, and in his Pride. But he knew she wouldn't want to leave her Pack. And she hated him. Not completely true. She hated his Pride. Even if it wasn't the same Pride as before.

But if this was all he could get, he'd take it. He could assuage his lion's concerns and fears about her safety and still get to see her occasionally. It wasn't what he wanted, but it was better than nothing.

She just couldn't see the effect she had on him. An old Marshall Tucker song came to mind as he watched her consider his proposal: *Can't you see what that woman, she been doin' to me.*

It seemed only his sister Luna was aware of how truly infatuated he was and how obsessed his lion had become with the tiny wolf. And it had become all that much worse after he'd left his mark on the back of her neck, after he'd claimed her in the way of his people to keep the wolves from Deathport from stealing her away and turning her into a breeder for their Pack.

That was all he'd planned originally; he'd just marked her to protect her until the laws were changed. But his already growing crush, his lion's insistence she was his mate from the moment he'd seen her on her property the night Callie had run away from Tammen, had grown exponentially. And he and his lion were going insane being away from her.

Hence, his constant creepy ass stalking.

"I don't have my phone on me," Emory said after a few agonizing moments.

Neither did he. He'd driven within a few miles then Shifted and made it to Big River territory by sticking to the trees. His lion didn't fear getting caught so late at night. But Eli did. Maybe if Emory agreed to let him see her a few times, it would keep his lion home.

"Meet me at Moe's after work. We'll have a couple of beers and exchange numbers," he offered as a solution since neither had brought their phones with them.

A smile ghosted her lips but then was gone just as quickly. It was a small smile, but he liked it; it had been just for him.

"I don't know, Eli." She sighed and looked over her shoulder at the houses behind her. Lights were coming on inside. Her Pack was stirring and it was just a matter of time before they realized Eli was on their land.

"Just an hour. That's all I'm asking for," he begged. And he had zero shame that he was begging. He'd drop to his knees right in front of her if it helped.

He might not have known Emory as well as her Pack or even the bears, but he knew something like that would scare her off. She was a straight shooter. She spoke her mind and did what she felt was right. Not just for herself, but her entire Pack. She was one of the most amazing women he'd ever met. And she hated being the center of attention.

She met his eyes and her pupils dilated. That was a good sign. It showed she was physically attracted to him, even if she had no desire to be with him. Then again, she *had* called him her mate.

Fighting every instinct to puff up and put on some stupid display of manliness to gain more of her attention, he shifted his weight onto his other foot.

"One hour," she said, her eyes narrowing. "That's all, Eli."

"One hour," he repeated.

"I get off at four."

"I'll meet you there."

She walked backward a few steps, and then her eyes dipped to his hand covered junk before she finally turned and walked at a fast clip back to her house. He cringed when he realized the quiet dude in their Pack was standing on his porch, watching them. Even as Emory got closer, the guy's eyes never left Eli.

Emory tilted her head up to him and said something too quiet for Eli's ears to pick up and the guy finally looked down at her and shook his head. He glanced up at Eli once more before turning and heading into his own house.

Holy shit. He had a date with Emory at four that night. He wouldn't have time to shower and change after work, but it wasn't like he'd be rolling around naked with her. Not yet anyway.

Maybe he'd promised she didn't owe him anything, and he'd promised to try to stay away from her territory, but Eli swore then and there, as he watched her tight little ass sway as she hurried away from him, that he'd do anything and everything to officially make her his. She already carried his mark; someday, he hoped he'd carry her heart.

****

What the hell was she thinking? She'd seriously just agreed to go out with Eli. It wasn't technically a date, more like a way to keep his lion to calm the hell down enough to keep from going all bat shit crazy. The last thing she wanted was him to lose his position in the Pride then have someone like Rhett take over again.

Who was she kidding? She'd wanted Eli since the night he'd shown up with Callie. Maybe she hadn't admitted it then, or even when he'd shown up at the bar, but yeah…there was something about him that just made her crazy.

But when he'd sank his damn teeth into the back of her neck, her lust turned into anger. He'd marked her, claimed her without permission. He hadn't bothered to ask her what she wanted. Okay, yeah. He'd more or less saved her from Deathport's clutches, but still. She'd wanted the choice in whether she was mated or not.

And just because neither of them said the words changed nothing about their status.

She almost tripped over her own feet as she stepped back into her house after telling Tristan to mind his own business. She *had* said the words out loud. She'd called him her mate when he'd said he'd been taking pills to try to make his lion chill out.

Had he caught that? He hadn't corrected her or puffed up with machismo at her words; maybe she'd get lucky and he'd think she was being sarcastic. Just because she was extremely attracted to him—and seeing the size of his package didn't help–and just because she permanently carried his mark didn't mean she had to be with him. She made her own rules. Lived her life the way she wanted.

And Eli didn't fit into that picture.

She looked around her little house, at her personal space filled with brightly colored pillows, bright yellow curtains, and feminine décor, and tried to picture his big body in there. He'd swallow the oxygen with his mere presence.

But he wouldn't want to live in her Pack. Not that she wanted that, of course. And she had no desire to live within Pride territory after everything they'd done to her Pack and what they'd put countless females through.

Eli wasn't like that, though. And he was changing things, making them better for his lionesses.

Emory sat heavily onto her futon and put her face in her hands. Who was she trying to convince? Who was she arguing with? Her wolf was fairly quiet, had done nothing but sit up and pay close attention the moment she'd sensed Eli nearby. She felt like she was going nuts having this weird back and forth in her own mind.

Every day around dawn, she'd felt him there, and she'd wondered if it'd been her imagination. She'd never seen him when she'd sought him in the morning, but she just knew he was there. But this morning, when she'd stepped out onto her porch, the wind had changed direction and wafted his scent straight to her nose. And he'd confirmed he'd been hanging around the last three weeks. How creepy was that that he'd been stalking her and none of her Pack had been any wiser. She needed to talk to Gray about security or going back to patrolling their perimeter each night like they used to back when Deathport was after her and Nova.

Surely, with an infant in their Pack, Gray would want to know they'd had a visitor every single night and no one had heard or scented him. How many times had something like that happened? How many times had Anson, the former and very dead Alpha of Deathport, stalked their line just waiting for his moment?

Emory could hear her Pack moving around inside their homes and tried to ignore the sounds of Callie and Micah making love already. She was going to end up having to take a page from Reed's book and put up some soundproof foam stuff to block out those sounds. She was happy for them, really she was, but it did nothing to calm her body after being so close to a very naked and very sexy Eli.

Taking a quick shower, she stared at herself in the mirror. Moe's was directly across the street from her job. She wouldn't have time to come back, change into regular clothes, and fix her hair and makeup. Then again, did she really want him to think she was doing all that for him? She'd told him she'd do this to calm his animal; she needed him to stay in power of his Pride and he couldn't do that if he went rogue.

She'd made sure he didn't think of this as a date, told him she'd only meet with him for one hour, but now she was considering packing a cuter top and some mascara in her purse.

No. She wasn't going to do a damn thing extra. She'd just show up in her work clothes, her hair would probably be crazy after tending to the farm and animal department all day, and she'd probably smell like a mixture of sweat and hay. This wasn't a date.

Damn it. How many times had she repeated that to herself?

Doors opened and closed and feet clomped on the hard wood of their porches. It was time for everyone to start their days. She'd always hated early mornings, hated waking to an alarm clock, but she'd rather the earlier shift than come home late at night when everyone else was here hanging out. She liked to be with her Pack. She loved to be around her family.

Where did Eli work? She knew literally nothing about him other than he was with Tammen and was now Alpha. And he was even sexier naked and all protective.

Shoving her foot into her tennis shoe with more force than was necessary, she struggled, as she had for the last few months, to get Eli out of her head and off her mind. No matter how hard she tried, though, he was always right there. She wondered stupid things about him, like what he wore to bed, what was his favorite food, and the most important question…

Did he care about any of the lionesses in his Pride? And she didn't mean like she cared about Reed or Tristan. He'd said he didn't have a mate, but was that because he wouldn't force himself on anyone? Had he had his eye on a female and she'd turned him down? Had any lionesses been sold to his Pride specifically for him?

Jealousy sent a green fog slithering through her belly at that thought. Which was stupid. Because he didn't belong to her.

Then again…

He had been hanging around her property, he had been watching over her, keeping her safe even before she'd known he was there. And he was obviously attracted to her. She'd caught him checking her out a few times before the war with Tammen. And she'd caught him checking out her chest when he thought she wasn't paying attention.

Emory grabbed her bag and locked the front door behind her. Callie and Nova would be home all day with little Rieka, and she didn't really care if either of them went into her home, but it was purely habit. And Nova had made it her business to replicate everyone's keys after she'd been with Gray a mere three months. It made it easier for her to break in to leave little trinkets and gifts she was always buying.

Tristan waited for her, leaning against the tail gate of his truck, his thick arms crossed over his chest. His brows were pulled low and he still looked pissed.

"I don't want to hear it, Tristan," she said as she passed.

"Stay away," was all he said. He rarely talked to anyone but her and he still didn't say more than two or three word sentences. It had been that way for the ten years she'd known him.

"Mind your business, Tris," she said, tossing her bag through her open door and turning on him. "I'm not stupid. I know what I'm doing."

"Tell Gray."

"I'm not telling Gray anything. Not yet," she whispered, looking around to make sure no one else was paying attention to their exchange.

"Morning," Nova called out from her front porch, Rieka nestled against her chest.

"Morning," Emory called back, forcing a smile before turning back to Tristan and shooting him a warning glare.

Emory waved at Nova and Callie as she left and headed into town. It would be the longest shift of her life. And the shortest. While she couldn't wait to spend the hour with Eli, she knew what she was doing was nothing short of playing with fire. She knew she should stay away from him, she knew she should tell Gray he'd been invading their property for weeks, but until she was sure of exactly what she was going to do about Eli, she would keep it to herself.

A blue Mustang sat at the intersection as she waited for the light to turn. She knew that vehicle. Eli. What was he doing now? She'd agreed to meet with him and even allowed herself to indulge in a few naughty thoughts about the size of his man meat, but she really didn't want him following her around everywhere. That was the best way to turn her off.

But he didn't follow her. He lifted his hand in a two-finger wave and turned the opposite direction when their light turned green. He was heading back into his Pride's territory.

He was heading back to the rest of the lions.

"Shit," she cursed in the quiet of her little car.

He was a freaking lion. They couldn't be anything. There was nothing she would or could do about Eli. Maybe it was okay for Micah to have fallen for a lioness, but she'd never wanted to be a mother and she knew lions had this deep seeded need to pop out as many kids as possible. And her luck, she'd have cubs, not pups. Definitely not something she wanted.

Turning up the radio, she tried to drown out thoughts of Eli or the sadness washing through her when she realized nothing could ever come from their meeting. She'd text him or whatever he needed to keep his lion stable, but that was all she had to offer him.

And that was the moment her wolf decided to perk up and throw in her own two cents.

Mate.

"I'm so screwed," Emory admitted aloud.

She was so very screwed.

Chapter Two

Eli's blue Mustang was already parked out front when Emory drove her car across the street and pulled into Moe's parking lot. There were quite a few cars and trucks there, actually. Unfortunately, she recognized a few of them. They would have an audience. And her meeting with Eli would get back to Gray pretty quickly.

They just might not have a full hour before her Pack came crashing the party.

With a deep breath, she closed her eyes and counted to three before pulling the door open. It took her eyes less than a half second to focus before she found Eli sitting alone at a table toward the back. There were two beers sitting on the table, one in front of him and one in front of the chair directly beside him.

Ignoring the eyes and questioning frowns being shot in her direction, she pushed through the crowd, grabbed the bottle of beer, and sat in the chair across from Eli. She wanted to sit close to him, wanted to press her thigh up against his, which was why she'd chosen the one furthest from him.

She was aware of how stupid that sounded, but it was the only thing she could think to do to quell the rumors that were sure to have already started.

Eli's mark tingled on the back of her neck when he smiled at her. She'd taken her hair out of the ponytail before leaving work in hopes of hiding it, but everyone knew it was there. Everyone could smell the change in her blood his mark made inside of her.

"Okay, you see me. I'm safe," she said, lifting the beer and taking a long swig. And then, of course, like the smooth lady she was, choked on the warm, bitter taste. "How long have you been sitting here? The beer's warm."

She sounded like a bitch. Maybe it would urge him to look elsewhere for his mate.

"Sorry. About an hour."

"You bought my beer an hour ago?" She pressed her lips into a thin line to hide the smile. Him waiting an hour was both pathetic and adorable.

He looked nervous when he shrugged and smiled sheepishly. "I got off work early." That was his only explanation. What she wanted to know, though, was whether he'd obsessed over their non-date all day like she had.

"I'll get you a new one," he said, standing quickly and rounding the table.

"Eli," she said, her hand wrapping around his wrist. He was so warm and she could feel the muscle in his forearm tighten at her touch. She released him quickly and folded her hands in her lap. They obviously couldn't be trusted around Eli. "It's fine."

"No. That was stupid. I should've known better." He started to move forward again and stopped. "Are you hungry?"

She shrugged. "I could eat." Screw it. If he was dead set on getting her a fresh beer and some munchies, she wasn't going to stop him.

"I'll get us some food."

He moved through the crowd with so much grace and she didn't bother hiding the fact she was watching his ass in his jeans. Damn. It was really a shame they'd met the way they had, because she'd love to just ogle him all day.

Someone chuckled and Emory glanced in that direction. Well, shit. Colton and Luke from the Blackwater Clan were there and had caught her checking Eli out. She frowned in their direction, but couldn't stay mad at Colton. He was one of her best friends and was so easy to like. He'd had a hard time since his dad had been murdered by the former Alpha of Tammen, but he didn't seem pissed that she was there with another lion. In fact, he seemed rather amused.

Which meant her entire Pack would know where she was and who she was with by the time she got home. If they didn't already know. There was a good chance Colton had already texted Gray or Reed to let them know she was there.

Turning her attention back to Eli, she smiled as he talked to Noah, his hands waving around before pointing in her direction. She stiffened when Noah's eyes met hers and he shook his head slowly.

Guess that told her how he felt about her little get together with the new Alpha.

Noah looked back at Eli, nodded once, and handed him two fresh beers. Eli turned back to Emory and made his way to their table, but Emory had a hard time ignoring the disapproving look the other Blackwater member was giving her from behind the bar. Yep. Her entire Pack would definitely know within a few minutes where she was because Noah had his phone in his hand and only stopped glaring at her to type something onto the screen.

Eli was smiling again as he carried the beers over, then frowned and looked over his shoulder, following her line of sight. When he looked back down at her, there was a brighter gold to his normally golden-brown eyes. He stood up straighter and seemed tense and she could smell fur wafting from him.

"What's wrong?" he asked, his voice deeper.

She shook her head and opened her mouth to tell him that Noah was probably tattling on her but did a double take. "Wait...are you getting all protective of me? Here? With my friends everywhere?"

Okay...that was kind of sweet. Completely misguided, as Colton and Luke would never let anything happen to her, nor would Noah, but maybe he didn't realize the bond they all had.

"You look scared."

He set the beer in front of her but didn't take his seat. Instead, he stood close to her, his eyes scanning the room,

"Oh my gosh, Eli. I'm not scared. I'm kind of unhappy that my Pack is probably getting a group text that I'm on a date with you, but I'm not scared."

His head quickly turned back to her and a smile spread across his face. "So this *is* a date?" he asked through his smile.

She rolled her eyes at him but couldn't hold back the smile. "No. But that's probably what Noah is telling everyone. Sit down. I'm fine. We're fine."

He pulled his chair back out and sat across from her, leaning onto his forearms and moving closer to her. "I like when you say *we*," Eli said. No. That wasn't him. There was way too much growl in his voice. That had been his lion and she wasn't here to entertain him, only placate him.

"You've seen I'm safe. Can I go now?"

For some reason, his lion watching her so closely flipped some kind of switch in her brain. Eli was hot, there was no doubt about her attraction for him nor the fact her wolf was ready to declare him all hers, but she didn't belong to anyone. Least of all a damn lion.

She pushed her chair back, but Eli leaned over the table further, reaching for her. "What happened? You looked like you were okay and now you look pissed. You worried what everyone will think of us being together?"

"We're not together, Eli." She stood, but then Eli was standing. "Eli–"

"Just stay. You said you'd give me an hour. That's all I'm asking for."

His eyes were back to normal and she couldn't sense his lion anymore. It was him begging her now, not his animal.

Looking around the room, she inwardly cringed at all the eyes on her. Whether they'd been watching the entire time or she'd just caught everyone's attention with their itty-bitty drama, she didn't know. But she didn't like being in the spotlight. Ever.

"Sit down," she whispered across the table. "Chill out. Stop talking about we and being together. I'm here to help you with your lion issue and that's it. And you promised you'd stay off our land if I came. That's it, Eli. That's how far this," she said, waving her hand back and forth between them, "will ever go."

He slowly sat on his chair, his eyes glued to her face. He held his hands out in front of him, palms out, as if he were trying to prove he wasn't a threat. She knew he wasn't. She didn't have an ounce of fear for him. What she feared was the way her body reacted to him, the way her wolf paced in her head when she was so near to him. What she feared was whether she had the strength to hold to her word and not allow him into her heart.

"I'm sorry. I'm just really nervous."

She finally sat and narrowed her eyes at him. "About what, Eli? This isn't a date. We're not mates."

"Yet you called me yours this morning."

Well, shit. He'd caught that. "I was being sarcastic," she lied.

Ugh. She hated this internal back and forth revolving around her feelings for him. It didn't matter, though, how she felt about him or how badly she wanted to crawl across the table and plant a big, wet kiss on his lips. He wanted more than she could give him.

"I don't think you were. But I promised you owed me nothing," he said, pulling his hands back and resting them on his lap under the table.

"You also promised to leave me alone and that's pretty much blown to crap," she said, taking a drink of her new beer. That time, it went down way smoother. His brow furrowed a little and there was this strange look of hurt in his eyes.

Eli had admitted his lion was obsessed with her. And Eli the man was definitely attracted to her. Perhaps he'd meant it when he said she owed him nothing, but if the look on his face was any indicator, her constant rejection was hurting him. And for some reason, she hated that. She hated that she was the one to cause that sad look on his face. She didn't want to be the one to hurt his feelings.

"I don't want kids," she blurted out before she lost her nerve. "I've never wanted to be a mother. Ever. So, if you're chasing after me in hopes of me popping out a slew of cubs, you're barking up the wrong tree."

"Lions don't bark," he said, a forced half smile on his lips.

She snorted, but shook her head. "You know what I meant."

"Why did you tell me that?" he asked, leaning forward and resting his forearm on the table.

"Because...if you think you'll just seduce me and we'll run off to your Pride and I'll just lay there with my legs open for you...nope, not happening, Eli."

"Did I say that was what I wanted from you?"

"No. But you didn't exactly tell me the real reason you marked me, either."

"Yes I did. I did it to stop Deathport."

"But, why?" she asked, narrowing her eyes at him.

He'd told her Pack he'd do everything he could to keep the females safe, but why hadn't he just stepped between her and the wolves? He was bigger than they were and she would've fought at his side. Hell, he could've just held them off until her friends and family saw she was in trouble and come to help.

He opened his mouth then shut it. And then he inhaled deeply and dropped his eyes to the table. "It was my lion," he admitted, raising his eyes to her face briefly before dropping them again. He'd done that a lot that morning, too, as if he were afraid to see her reaction.

"Why?" she breathed out, leaning closer.

His eyes closed and he inhaled deeply again, his broad chest rising and falling with the deep breath. "Because he chose you. You're my...fuck." He looked at her then, locked eyes with her. "You're my mate, Emory. My real mate. I'm sorry. I swear I tried to stop him, tried to talk him down. And I still swear you owe me nothing."

The air was caught in her lungs and her heart raced painfully. Her wolf had declared the same damn thing earlier in the day. But she didn't want this. She didn't. Eli was hot and sweet, but she didn't want a mate. And she sure as hell didn't want to be tied to a lion.

"Nothing I just said makes any difference?" she asked, fully aware of how breathy she sounded.

"No."

"I'll never change my mind, Eli. I don't want to be a mom."

"I don't care."

Well, shit. What was she supposed to say to that? "How would this even work?" she asked.

"What do you mean?"

"I'm pretty sure my Pack won't allow you to stay in our territory, and I have no desire to live with the same assholes who tried to steal one of my family members and had no problem trying to kill anyone who got in the way. Hell, your Pride killed Colton's dad."

"No. Rhett did that. Just him. Not my Pride, not me. Just Rhett," Eli said, leaning further onto the table. He didn't drop his eyes again. Just held hers and waited for her to process everything. He opened his mouth again but snapped it shut. And then that sad look was back. "Shit," he breathed.

"Exactly," she said.

"No. Your Pack is here," he said, glancing over her shoulder then looking back at her.

Damn Noah. Why couldn't he just leave it alone and let her make up her own mind? Instead, she turned to find every single member of her Pack, including Nova and Callie standing near the doorway, staring at her as if she'd lost her mind. Except Tristan. His look was a combination of gloat and anger as he glared at Eli.

"Guess an hour was asking too much," Eli said and nodded, as if telling her to go ahead with her family.

"No. We still have forty minutes," she said, glancing at the time on her phone.

She might have originally agreed to this non-date to keep Eli's animal calm, but now, it was the principle of the whole thing. Her Pack had fought for her, for Nova and Callie, for *all* females to have the power over their own lives. And they weren't taking her choice away, regardless of how they felt about Eli and Tammen.

"Whatcha doin', Em?" Reed asked, pulling a chair out and sitting between Emory and Eli.

"Minding my own business. You should try it," she shot back at him, giving him a tight-lipped smile.

"Eli," Gray said with a nod of his head, his voice low and a little growly.

"Can you guys give us some privacy, please?" Emory asked, turning to look up at Gray.

"They can hang out," Eli said, winking at her when she turned to frown at him. "Have a seat. Food should be here soon."

"Don't have a seat. He didn't order enough for everyone," Emory said.

"You guys on a date?" Nova asked in her usual teasing tone, but there was obvious trepidation in the slight crease of her brow.

"Where's Rieka?" Emory asked when she realized the entire Pack was there but not the baby.

"With my dad. Told him we were meeting you for dinner. At least, that's what I thought," Nova said, her eyes flicking between Emory and Eli.

"And why would you think that?" Emory asked.

Nova jerked her chin toward Reed.

Reed raised his hands and widened his eyes. "Technically, I said we were going to *crash* Emory's dinner. I said nothing about joining her."

"You're a jerk. You couldn't have my back for once?" Emory asked, fighting the urge to poke out her bottom lip.

Now that her non-date had been officially ruined, she really wished she'd made better use of the short time they'd had together. All they'd done was bicker a little. Not true. She'd told him a few reasons of why they couldn't be together and he'd given her sad eyes and more or less tried to beg her with just his expression to give them a chance.

Reed's light brows pulled together and he leaned forward, his elbow resting on the table as he got in her bubble. "I'm here *because* I have your back," he said softly, but he knew Eli could hear him. Every Shifter in the place could hear every word of their conversation since they weren't exactly being quiet.

"I'm fine, Reed. You guys, we're just talking," Emory said, looking each person in the eye but avoiding Tristan all together. He was the only one of their family who knew the entirety of her past, knew why she'd been on her own when they'd found each other. She knew why he was being so protective, and she knew why he was pissed she was with Eli alone.

Gray pulled a few chairs up to the small table, and now the entire Pack was squished in around her, their eyes pretty much glued to Eli.

"I could've sworn you promised Emory you'd stay away from her. Maybe it's just my imagination, but didn't you tell her she owed you nothing?" Gray said, the scent of fur growing by the second.

"I did. And she still owes me nothing," Eli said.

"So why, then, have you been in my territory every single fucking night?" Gray asked, leaning forward, his eyes too blue.

How did he know Eli had been there? She hadn't said anything to anyone, except...

Slowly turning her eyes to Tristan, she narrowed them and furrowed her brows so deep she wondered if she wouldn't get a permanent crease. The fucking traitor had told their Alpha about Eli stalking Emory every night.

"Thanks, Tris," she muttered, still glaring at him.

"Not right," Tristan said, not bothering to even pretend to be apologetic at all.

"I'm sorry," Eli said, his eyes bouncing to Emory for a second before turning back to Gray. He needed to make sure he held Gray's gaze or it would show either weakness or deceit. And neither would go over well with her Alpha. "It was my lion."

"Explain," Gray said, not bothering to lean back or relax.

Nova placed her hand on Gray's forearm and squeezed lightly. That seemed to help calm Gray a little, but not nearly enough. If he got too pissed and Shifted, there was a good chance they'd have a full out brawl right there in the middle of Moe's. She'd spotted a couple of Tammen lions when she'd first gotten there; no way they'd let Big River Pack attack their Alpha without jumping in to protect him.

Eli looked to Emory, but she couldn't help him here. She only knew as much as he'd told her. And she'd never been out of control of her animal, had no idea what it felt like to completely lose herself to her wolf. She had no idea what he was going through or truly how to help him, other than this little meeting and the text messages he'd requested.

"After my lion marked Emory, he became possessed," Eli said, turning to Gray. He told her Alpha what he'd told her that morning, about how he'd tried to drug his lion to keep him home at night, but nothing was working. "I promised her I'd stay away. And I'm really trying. That's why we're here."

"How is that staying away from her?" Reed asked.

"I'm hoping if my lion sees her occasionally, maybe if he knows she's safe, he'll stop with the creepy stalker crap," Eli said, his eyes bouncing to Emory's before returning to Gray's.

"It's beyond creepy stalker crap, Eli. You're invading my territory. How am I supposed to take that? I've got a pup. Your Pride has already attacked once." Gray sat back, but Emory could see he wasn't relaxed by the way a muscle ticked in his cheek.

"My Pride under Rhett's orders. We just want to live our lives without any extra bullshit," Eli said. He didn't shift in his chair under all the attention he was getting from her Pack. He didn't drop his gaze to the table or his hands, didn't tense up or look to see if his Pride was paying attention to the confrontation. These were all good things, as it kept her Pack from going all feral on him, but it made her wonder about his true motives when it came to her.

Why not just tell them whatever was going on between he and Emory was none of their business? Why not just come up with some better excuse or lie as to why he'd been on their property so much? Because admitting he was losing a battle with his lion over Emory showed weakness, especially for an Alpha of a known aggressive Pride.

"Are the rest of them following your orders?" Callie asked, leaning into Micah's side.

Emory was actually surprised at how quiet the Second in the Pack had been the entire time, but he hadn't stopped glaring at Eli and his eyes were bright blue. After learning Micah was part coyote, his constant snarling at everyone but Callie made more sense. But it also made Emory nervous. She'd assumed he'd be the first one to insult Eli, threaten him, something. Callie really had made a huge difference in Micah's life, but Emory could smell the potent scent of his fur, even from across the table.

Eli ghosted her with a glance, but looked away quickly before he set Micah off. Good idea. Just because Micah was restraining himself and his animal right now didn't mean he wouldn't lose his shit if either side of him felt their former enemy was paying too much attention to his mate.

"They are. For the most part. There have been a few challenges, but those who didn't like the new rules have left," Eli answered, glancing up at Callie then away again.

"The women are free?" Callie asked.

"All of them. They have the choice to stay or go and they no longer have to stay with a male unless they want to. A few have moved in with me and my sister," he answered.

Emory's brows popped up to her hairline. He had a sister? Emory carried his mark and her wolf had declared him her mate, yet she knew literally nothing about him other than the size of his dick and how he looked without clothes.

"Easier access to your harem," Reed said, his blond brows pulled together.

"They are not my lionesses. I only have one mate," he said, and then closed his mouth so fast his teeth clacked together.

One by one, it seemed Eli's words registered to her Pack and they each turned to look at her with wide eyes. Except Tristan. He looked pissed. But she had no idea how much of that anger was for Eli and how much was for Emory.

Gray blew out a rush of air and dragged his hand roughly down his face. "I still can't have you sneaking around my property every night. I have a fucking mate and a baby. If I catch you out there, it'll be a fucking fight."

"Wait a minute," Nova said, waving her hands in the air as if trying to get her mate's attention even though he was sitting right beside her. "He just admitted they're mates. You can't just make him stay away from her."

"As long as you and Rieka are there–"

"And Callie," Micah cut in, his eyes still locked on Eli.

"I don't want anyone from Tammen or fucking Deathport anywhere near my fucking territory."

"Yeah, but if they're mates, you know damn well it's almost impossible to stay away from each other. Or are you trying to suggest she leave?" Nova asked, crossing her arms. "Because as Alpha's mate, I veto."

"You don't get to veto just because you're the Alpha's mate," Reed said with a slow shake of his head.

"If he ever wants another blow job for the rest of his life, I do."

All the men looked horrified as they turned to Gray to see what his answer would be.

"Would you guys shut the hell up? This is between us, not you," Emory said, shooting every single member of her Pack an incredulous look. "No one said we're mates."

"He said you were his," Nova said, pointing at Eli without looking at him. "And I know damn well that stuff is never one sided. Has your wolf claimed him yet?"

"Nova, oh my gosh. Will you stop?" Emory's ears burned with embarrassment. She had a feeling she resembled a freaking tomato as everyone watched her and waited for her answer.

"He did mark you," Nova said with a shrug, as if it should be totally obvious.

"That doesn't mean anything," Emory said, but she was running out of steam.

This had already been uber confusing before Noah had narced her out and invited her Pack to crash her non-date with the lion who was also waiting for her answer now. She'd already told him she had no desire to be a mom. She never wanted to get pregnant or pop out pups or cubs or whatever. But he hadn't seemed swayed by that.

And, yeah, her animal kind of claimed him, but she really didn't want to divulge that information in a crowded bar with even the Blackwater guys leaning a little closer and trying their damnedest to pretend they weren't listening to the conversation.

But if she didn't, would they leave Eli alone? Would they stop with the interrogation? Or would it just get worse?

****

Eli all but leaned forward in anticipation of Emory's answer. He'd pointed out to her she'd already referred to him as her mate back at her home, but she'd yet to admit it since. Now, her Pack was pressing her, waiting for her answer just like he was. They'd turned the full attention away from him and were staring at her, a small smile on Nova's and Callie's lips, scowls or looks of confusion on the guys' faces.

"This is bullshit," Emory said, standing so quickly her chair wobbled before Reed grabbed the back to keep it upright. She jabbed her finger at Reed. "You've got my back? Really, Reed?" Her eyes went to each member of her Pack. "I found someone who interests me yet here you all are, cock blocking. Maybe he is my mate. I don't know. But you guys make sure you stand right in the middle so I'll never know for sure."

She turned and stormed off, her dark hair swinging behind her.

And then all eyes turned to Eli.

"You better go after her," Nova said, grabbing Emory's purse from the back of her chair and passing it over the table.

"I'll go talk to her," Reed said, raising from his seat.

"No you won't. You'll sit right there or I promise, I'll kick your ass myself," Nova said, the hand holding Emory's bag still outstretched as she turned to frown at Reed.

Reed held his hands out in surrender and lowered back into his seat. "I'm just saying, if I'm the one who pissed her off, maybe I should go apologize."

"We all pissed her off," Callie said.

"She shouldn't have been here alone, anyway," Micah, Big River's Second said, his eyes too blue to pass as human.

"She wasn't alone. Look around, Micah. Our friends are here. Our allies are here. No one would touch her," Callie said, pointing out various members of the Blackwater Clan, the Ravenwood Pride, and a few others Eli only knew in passing.

Eli hesitated only a second before taking the bag from Nova's hand, dipping his head once, and rushing through the crowd of people, ignoring the eyes on him as he damn near knocked people to the ground to get to Emory.

The second he was through the door, he was scanning the parking lot for the tiny female his lion was yearning for. She stood leaned against her car, her profile to him, her arms crossed over her chest as she stewed over everything that had happened in less than twenty-four hours.

She didn't look up as he crunched across the gravel, forcing his steps to stay slow instead of sprinting to her side like he really wanted to. When had he become such a freaking sap? He was far from a virgin, had attempted a few relationships through the years, but he'd never felt so damn enamored with a woman in his twenty-eight years of life. Hell, enamored wasn't a strong enough word for what he felt looking at this petite wolf.

"This isn't going to work," Emory said when he stopped in front of her and held her bag out to her.

"What isn't going to work?"

She looked up at him and anger and heartache warred within him at the shimmer of moisture in her turquoise eyes. Seriously, who had eyes like that? And how the hell did humans not realize she wasn't one of them with her striking features, the sharp cut of her cheekbones, her grace?

And there he was obsessing over her appearance when she was trying to have some kind of heart to heart with him. Maybe he wasn't so different from the rest of his Pride. Her looks were what had originally caught his attention. Her hips and tits were what had caught his lion's. Now, both sides of him couldn't seem to drink her in enough.

Eli turned to the side a little when his pants grew tighter. Fuck. He had to get this shit under control. If she even thought he wanted her for nothing more than her beauty she'd be gone in a heartbeat. And that truly wasn't the only reason he wanted her. She was funny. She was strong and sassy and had no problem telling off anyone who fucked with her or her family. She was smart and obviously self-sufficient and independent if she'd been able to go her whole life without being claimed by a male.

Well, at least until his lion had taken advantage of her situation with the wolves.

"All of it, Eli. And could you please stop staring at my boobs?" she said, snapping her fingers in his face.

His eyes jerked to hers. He hadn't even realized he'd been checking her out, even as he'd internally chastised himself for paying so much attention to her physical traits.

Thinking quickly, he shook his head and pointed at a spot on her shirt. "I wasn't. You have a stain or something."

She frowned, looked down at her shirt, then smirked up at him. "You're a terrible liar," she said, but there wasn't much force behind her words.

Okay, so she'd caught him ogling her, but at least she wasn't going off on him or taking off. In fact, it looked like she was trying to hide her smile as she pressed those sexy lips into a thin smile and looked away.

He had to get them back on track before he said or did something stupid, like getting caught checking her out again.

"Why do you think this won't work?" he asked, taking a risk and lifting his hand to push hair from her face that the wind had blown.

Her eyes softened when he'd brushed the hair away, but she schooled her face and crossed her arms again. "Did you not catch what just happened, Eli? The second my Pack got wind that we were here together every single one of them came barging in and placed themselves between us. And how would it work if you and I admitted we were mates? Would you live in my Pack? I don't think I could stomach living in your Pride."

Eli shrugged up his shoulders. "Why not? It's not like it was before." It really wasn't. He'd made sure of that. Those males who'd refused to change were told to leave. Everything had been good for the last couple of months, even if it was a little tense at times.

"Why not? Seriously? Your Pride, all of them, attacked my Pack, Eli. You can pretend they did it because they were given Alpha's orders, but that didn't seem to work on you. Those guys had just as much choice as you did."

"Did you happen to notice not a single one of your friends were killed?" he asked, a little anger creeping into his voice. "Not all lions are dicks, Em." She seemed a little surprised at his use of her nickname, but he didn't let that stop his tirade. "There were enough of us that your entire Pack could've been wiped out. That didn't happen. Yeah, you had the bears, but you were still outnumbered. The assholes who wanted to hurt you are dead. Those left behind just want to live their lives as normally as possible."

"How many of your buddies were happy about losing their harem?" she asked, her angry tone now matching his.

He opened his mouth then shut it. Eli couldn't lie to her, but he really didn't want to tell her the full truth, either. He was trying to tell her all the great things about his Pride and why she should consider joining him at home, but there was no way she'd agree to come onto his territory if he knew the full extent of the backlash he'd received when he'd enforced the new laws.

"That's what I thought," she said, coming to her own conclusion at his silence. "I think you're awesome, Eli. I really do. I just…" She shook her head. "I'll text you a few times a week, but please stay off our property. Gray knows you've been around now and he'll be watching for you. I don't want anything to happen to you."

She dropped her head and fumbled through her purse until she found her keys. She played with them for longer than was necessary to locate the fob to unlock her door. Eli took a huge chance, cupped her face, and tilted her head up to his.

Lowering his head, he pressed his lips to hers before she had a chance to slug him in the jaw. She tensed for a second, but then her lips were moving against his, so soft and full like he'd imagined they would be. A soft whimper escaped her, then she pulled away, leaving him reeling. Holy shit. That had been nothing more than a chaste touch of the lips and he was about to hyperventilate.

Her fingertips went to her lips and she stared wide-eyed at him. She'd felt it. She'd felt that same connection, those weird little zaps of energy where they'd touched. He'd been right. His fucking lion had been right.

Emory was his mate.

He'd try his damnedest to stay away from her, to give her some time and space to admit to they belonged together. Unfortunately, his lion was begging for more. Staying away from her was going to be the hardest thing he'd ever done in his life.

****

Emory laid in bed and stared at the dark ceiling. Holy hell. He'd kissed her. Eli had actually kissed her. There'd been no tongue or anything more than a gentle touch, but her heart was still racing. And her wolf hadn't shut up since.

Had she had any doubts about his place in her heart, they'd all been put to rest. She wanted him so bad. And yet she still couldn't figure out how the hell they could possibly make it work. Gray was pissed at the news Eli had been on their property every single fucking morning, but what could she do about that? Nothing.

And, honestly, there was this little part of her that kind of liked that his lion was watching out for her. Not that she couldn't take care of herself, but just like with her Pack, she had someone who cared enough about her safety to risk his own life.

That was exactly what he was doing, too. Because had Gray or Micah found him before she had, they would've challenged him. The entire Pack might have gone after him. After what the Tammen Pride had done a few months ago, there was a good chance they would've killed him.

The thought of Eli dead did something to her stomach and heart. Both hurt equally. Both felt like someone was taking a sledgehammer to them. She needed Eli alive and well. Even if she couldn't have him.

But she wanted him, damn it. So bad. There had to be a way to include him, even if at arm's distance. There had to be a way to fit him into her life like a puzzle piece.

She schemed and plotted and yet there were holes in every single plan she came up with. She was a grown ass woman and she was trying to think of ways to sneak around to be with her damn mate. And no matter how hard she tried to fight it, regardless of whether she'd run out instead of admitting it to her Pack, Eli, Alpha of Tammen Pride, was her mate.

Frustration was keeping her wide awake. Pushing from bed, she wandered onto the front porch and leaned against the railing. Now she wished she'd done like Nova and Gray and got a chair or bench for her deck.

Everything had a silvery-blue haze to it from the full moon. Was Eli awake? Was he staring at the same moon and thinking about her? And when did she become this kind of woman who wondered whether a man was pining after her?

She'd always been a little opposed to the whole mate thing. She wanted to just meet a guy, fall in love, and build a life with him. She didn't want the universe to choose for her. She sure as hell didn't want her animal to pick who she'd call her own. Yet, there she was, wishing she could talk to a man she barely knew. She wanted more than just a press of his lips. She wanted to be in his arms. She wanted to feel his hands on her.

Great. Now she was turning herself on with thoughts of Eli's big hands. And they were big. Just like every other part of him. He was so broad and strong, his legs thick and corded with muscles, his shoulders would fill a doorway, and he was over a foot taller than her. Then again, everyone was taller than her five-foot-one. She always felt like a kid next to the rest of her Pack. Even Callie was taller than Emory by a few inches.

But her small stature had never kept her from fighting for herself. It had never hindered her from taking care of herself when males tried to claim her. So why did it seem like neither she nor her wolf fought all that hard against Eli when he'd clamped his teeth down on her neck? She'd fought, but had she really? Had she put much effort at all in trying to get away from him?

Emory stayed on her porch, even as the moon moved across the sky. She was off work tomorrow. She'd have all day to dwell on everything that had happened that day. She'd have nothing to do but think.

Who was she kidding? Callie and Nova would be there with the baby. Emory knew full well her friends would be dying for some details, especially Nova. She'd beg for more and file it away in her little romance folder in her brain.

There was no romance. Okay. Maybe there had been a little. The way he'd watched her at Moe's, the way he'd instantly gotten protective when he'd thought she was afraid, the way he'd kissed her…

Emory released the girliest sounding sigh of her entire life at the memory of his lips. He was big and covered in tattoos, yet he'd been so sweet and gentle. He hadn't pushed for more. Hadn't held her in place when she'd pulled away.

She really hadn't wanted to pull away. She'd wanted to climb him like a tree, wrap her legs around his waist, and deepen the kiss. But she'd known her Pack could come out at any moment and that would've sucked. Gray was already pissed at the news of Eli's invasion of his property; surely, he would've been irate to find them making out in the parking lot.

But why? Why should he care who she fooled around with? It wasn't his business. Emory had been fully supportive of Nova when she'd arrived, even though her presence could have and did cause a little drama.

Emory had been fully supportive of Callie and Micah when she'd come crashing into their territory, literally. She'd plowed over their fire pit and destroyed quite a few of their lawn chairs when she was trying to get away from the Tammen Pride. Yet, when Micah had claimed her as his mate, Emory was behind them all the way. She'd never pointed out how dangerous it was to have the lioness on their land, never pointed out that their union could and did cause a war. She'd never pointed out how detrimental Callie's presence on their land could be with a pregnant female living there.

Yet, every single one of her Pack sure as hell seemed to be one hundred percent against her even dating Eli. Actually, Nova had seemed intrigued, not pissed. She'd even spoken up against Gray when he'd tried to tell Eli and Emory to stay away from each other.

She needed to talk to Nova. Callie, too. They were her sisters, her only female friends. And they'd had rocky starts to their relationships. Maybe they'd have an idea of how to make it work.

And she realized, even though she'd told Eli it couldn't, she wanted it to work. She wanted *them* to work. She wanted to see what they could be. She wanted to see where this little mating thing could go.

She wanted Eli.

Eli. Mate.

Her wolf wanted him just as badly.

Chapter Three

Emory's knees bounced as she sat on the couch, listening to the guys starting up their trucks and heading off for the day. She needed to talk to the girls, but she really didn't feel like dealing with Tristan or anyone else. She couldn't take the looks or questions right now. She was screwed up in her own head without the extra crap from them.

The second the rumble of the vehicles faded to nothing, she jumped up and ran from her house, heading straight for Nova's. "Callie! Girl meeting," she called out as she jogged to the first house in a row.

Callie was on Nova's porch and stepping through the door within seconds of Emory.

Nova bounced Rieka in her arms, a confused frown pulling her dark brows together.

"What's up? Eli come again this morning?" Nova asked.

"No. I don't know. I don't think so," Emory blurted out as she paced the small space. She smiled down at Rieka as she passed, then resumed her hindered march.

"Girl, what's got your panties twisted?" Nova said, setting her baby in the little pink bassinet. She grabbed two more mugs and filled them with coffee before passing them out.

Emory clutched the ceramic like a lifeline, but finally stopped her pacing and leaned against the counter.

"I want Eli," she blurted out.

Callie and Nova frowned at each other, but it was Nova who spoke. As usual. "Duh. We know that."

"Yeah, no...I mean...shit." She'd wanted to talk to them but now she couldn't get her thoughts together. Even as she tried to form the words to come out of her mouth, she couldn't quite make the words make sense inside her head. "I mean, I don't know how we can do this."

"Do what, exactly?" Callie asked, her eyes narrowing.

"Omg, Callie. I'm not a virgin, if that's what you're asking." Emory snorted and smiled. Callie had been a twenty-two-year-old virgin when she and Micah had gotten together. Apparently, she'd thought Emory was asking sex advice.

"Sorry. I'm just trying to figure out what exactly you're trying to say," Callie said, holding her hands out.

"Yeah. What are you trying to get at, because I was kind of thinking the same thing? If it doesn't refer to sex, what *it* are you talking about?" Nova said, sitting in the chair beside her daughter's bassinet and looking down with the softest expression.

"The whole thing. All of it. A relationship. This whole mate thing," Emory said, straightening and pacing again. "He's a lion."

"Yeah. So am I," Callie said, frowning up at Emory.

"He's the Alpha of Tammen, Callie. Not some lioness running for her life. He's leading the same damn Pride who tried to take you. The same Pride who tried to kill us."

"None of our people died," Nova pointed out with brows raised. "That's got to mean something."

"Right. None of ours died. Theirs did. And you saw how many lions and Deathport wolves were here," Callie said.

"That's another thing. Why didn't he just fight beside me instead of marking me?" Emory said, jabbing a finger at the mark in question currently tingling on her neck.

Nova shrugged. "Maybe his lion didn't think it through. Or maybe it was his way of forcing himself on you. Or maybe, it was just a spur of the moment thing and neither side of Eli thought they had any other options. You'll have to ask him that one."

"I did. I didn't like the answer," Emory admitted, then told them what he'd said at the bar.

Nova's eyes did that squishy, soft thing they always did when it came to love and romance. "Sounds like fate to me," she said with smile.

"Oh, bullshit. It sounds like another male trying to force himself on me."

"A male you've already admitted to wanting," Nova said.

Callie pointed at Nova like she'd made a valid point.

"You never answered yesterday. Is he your mate?" Callie asked, leaning forward a little, her elbow on her knee, her chin propped on her hand.

Emory turned to Callie and opened her mouth, did that fish thing where her lips kept puckering around words, then closed it. Yeah. He was. Undoubtedly. Even as she spoke with her Pack sisters, her wolf was pacing in her head chanting Eli's damn name, and it was driving her insane.

She stopped pacing, wrapped her arms around her middle, and dropped her head. "Yes," she whispered.

"What was that?" Nova asked. Even without looking up at her, Emory could tell Nova was smiling.

Emory raised her head and looked straight at Nova. "Yes. Eli is my mate. And I know nothing about him other than his first name, he's Alpha of a shitty Pride, and he has a big dick."

Callie and Nova both stared at her with wide eyes. And in usual Nova fashion, her smile grew wide and she leaned forward. "Really? Eli has a big dick? Like, you saw it?"

"Yesterday morning. He was naked when he came out of the woods. And, yeah…he's got a nice package."

Nova looked at Callie with her brows to her hairline, then both women burst into laughter with Nova clapping her hands together. Rieka fussed a little at the noise, so they both quickly quieted.

"Sorry, baby girl," Nova whispered down at her daughter. "But this is juicy stuff." Nova turned her attention back to Emory. "What do you need from us, Em?"

"Advice?" Emory said, shaking her head. "I don't know what to do. Gray doesn't want him here. I'm terrified to go there."

"Why?" Callie asked.

"What do you mean why? You lived there. You know what it's like," Emory said, twisting her face into her best *duh* expression.

"I know what it used to be like. That was when Rhett was running things. He's dead. Brent's dead. Eli's in charge now, and he put himself on the line to protect you," Callie said.

"All he did was bite me," Emory said, anger rising again.

"Against his Alpha's orders. You were supposed to be delivered to Deathport. You know that. He put himself between the wolves and you and protected you with that bite. And I truly believe if you told him to eff off, he would. He might still stalk you, but I don't think he'd ever really push you for more."

"Romeo stalked Juliet," Nova said with a nod.

"And they lived for, what, three days after? Not the best analogy," Emory said.

"Good point," Nova said with a sharp nod, but she was pressing her lips into a thin line and failing miserably to hide her smile.

"This isn't funny," Emory said, but she, too, was having a hard time fighting the humor.

"Why don't you just talk to him about all this," Callie offered. "Maybe try dating and see where that goes."

"Because every time I'm around him all I want to do is throw myself at him. And that pisses me off so I end up listing every reason we can't be together and acting like a bitch."

"Hey, some guys like that," Nova said, then put her hands out when Emory shot her a look. "Callie's right, though. Talk to him. And stop making stupid excuses. If you're mated, for real mated and not that crap that they used to do to Callie and the rest of the women, there's no use fighting it. You'll both end up miserable."

"He said he's been losing the battle with his lion and keeps attacking his own Pride," Emory said, crossing the room and dropping onto the couch beside Callie.

"Not good," Callie said.

"Yeah. No shit," Emory said, then nudged Callie with her shoulder to soften her bitchy attitude. "You know, I…" Shit. She didn't want to admit all this out loud.

"What?" Callie said, turning and lifting a knee onto the couch to look at Emory.

"I think there was a part of me that wanted Eli to mark me. Like, I knew I'd fight that stuff, so my wolf was all excited that he took the initiative. Which is stupid, because I'm no damsel. I've taken care of myself for a long time. I've run away from stuff like that. I've run away from men like him."

"Explain," Nova said.

Emory shrugged. More shit she really didn't want to get into. More stuff she really didn't want to tell anyone else. Tristan knew everything and now he was overly protective to the point he might just literally place himself between Emory and Eli.

"I don't want some Neanderthal putting me in chains," Emory said softly, memories flying through her head fast enough to make her dizzy.

"What happened?" Callie asked, and the pity in her voice snapped Emory out of it.

"Nothing. It doesn't matter. We're supposed to be talking about the Eli thing. How do I have him without pissing off every single person we know? I don't want Gray mad at me. But I've got to be straight with you–I don't know how much longer I can take my wolf in my head like this."

"Ooooh. I remember those days," Nova said, nodding over and over. "Oh yeah. She about drove me nuts. I didn't hear a word from her for years and then *boom*. She's nonstop cheering Gray's name. It was weird when she'd do that during sex, like she was some kind of voyeur or something."

Emory stared at Nova in mild shock, then opened her mouth and released a loud laugh. "You're nuts, you know that?" Emory said.

"Yep. And you love it."

"I purred the first time Micah touched me," Callie blurted out.

Nova fanned herself. "Callie Kitty, tell me more."

"No!" Callie said around a laugh. "That was embarrassing enough. All I'll say is she hasn't stopped purring since. What I'm trying to say is it's apparently normal for our animals to go a little crazy until we give them what they want," Callie said.

"Tease," Nova pouted.

"Perv," Callie fired back.

"You girls are literally no help," Emory said, crossing her arms and sitting back against the futon cushion.

"We just told you what you need to hear. It's normal for them to be noisy until they get their mates. Your wolf won't shut up, but it won't be so bad after," Nova said.

Dropping her head back against the couch, Emory closed her eyes and listened to her wolf pine for Eli. Callie seemed to think Emory should give the Pride a chance while they both thought she should try dating Eli and letting it progress naturally. Both scenarios scared her and she knew it would piss off her Pack.

What about the women from his Pride? Would she be hated because she stole one of their males? Most of the women didn't want to be there, but the lionesses who chose that life, the ones who were attached to Rhett, probably felt like Eli was theirs now. And here she was, a wolf from a rival Pack swooping in and stealing their man.

"What are the chicks like?" Emory asked, sitting up to look at Callie.

"What?" Callie asked, confused by the sudden change of topic.

"The females at Tammen. What are they like?"

Callie's brows raised high and she shrugged. "There were a lot who were miserable. They didn't want to be there. We didn't talk all that much. Rhett's mates were jerks. They treated everyone else like crap. Why?" Callie glanced at Nova and winked. "Are you thinking about living there?"

"Hold on. I was all excited for you, but I didn't really think about you leaving here. I don't know if I like the thought of you living in the Pride," Nova said, her tone uncharacteristically serious.

"Well, he can't live here, Nova."

"Sure he can," Nova said.

"Yeah. I'm sure Gray would just love that. Tell you what. You text him right now and ask him how he'd feel. If he gives the green light, I'll go to Eli right now and tell him I want him."

"No you won't," Nova said, narrowing her eyes.

"Yep. We'll make it a bet. He says sure, I'll go find Eli right now. You can even come with me as a witness. If he says no..." Emory tapped a finger to her lips like she was thinking hard. "If he says no, then you have to not only admit you're wrong and I'm always right, but you're the DD for the next three trips to Moe's."

"DD?" Callie asked.

"Designated driver," Emory said with a wide, triumphant smile. She already knew exactly what Gray was going to say, so she knew she was safe and would have a sober driver the next three times they went into town to drink.

"Oooh," Callie said. "Yeah. I kind of like that bet. I'm tired of being the chauffeur," she admitted.

"Fine. Let's find out," Nova said, but she didn't sound so confident as she pulled her phone from her back pocket and tapped the screen over and over. And then they all waited.

It was three seconds later Nova's phone dinged with a reply. Nova's face fell and she frowned up at Emory.

"What? He didn't welcome him in with open arms?" Emory said, her eyes wide, her brows pulled high with mock surprise.

"He said, and I quote, fuck no." She shoved her phone back in her pocket. "You know, that wasn't very nice. You know I went nine months without drinking when I was pregnant."

Emory shrugged. "Should've listened to me. Because...what?"

"I'm wrong and you're always right," Nova grumbled.

"I love hearing those words," Emory said with a wide smile.

She might be stressed out and confused, but she could always count on her girls to make things seem a little easier.

"Okay, fine. So you were right. What are you going to do, then?" Nova asked, crossing her arms and looking every bit the petulant child.

The question of the century. So, maybe it wasn't that big, but it sure as hell felt like it. She wanted to be happy. And she knew being with Eli would make her happy. Or, at least, she hoped it would. She'd never know if she didn't give them a shot.

"I told him I didn't want kids. Like ever. And he seemed okay with it."

Callie and Nova exchanged a look.

"What?" Emory asked, looking from one to the other.

"Lions have a need to procreate," Callie said.

"Or they were *taught* they needed to procreate," Emory corrected. "Do you want to be a mom?" she asked the lioness.

"Yeah. Someday. I'm not ready now. We give birth to multiples. I'm not really ready to pop out two or three cubs—"

"Or pups," Nova cut in.

"Or pups," Callie corrected herself. "But maybe someday."

"Maybe. So, even though you were raised to believe it was your job to populate the Earth with a ton of Callie juniors, you're not ready for a family. He said that was fine. I have to believe him until he gives me a reason to think otherwise."

"Never? Like, you never want kids?" Nova asked, her brows pulled together.

Emory shook her head and stashed that conversation with the rest she didn't want to have. "Nope. Never."

"Huh," was all Nova could come up with. That was fine with Emory. She didn't want to discuss it any further, anyway.

"Back on subject, girls," Emory said, clapping her hands. "What. Do. I. Do?"

"I say date. Get to know each other. Spend time together and don't worry about what everyone else thinks. I always liked Eli. He was good to everyone and tried to protect the lionesses as much as he could," Callie said.

"I'll take care of Gray. Maybe don't bring him here for your first date, but yeah. Like Callie said, get to know each other without all the extra crap from the guys," Nova said.

"What about his Pride?"

Nova shrugged. Callie shrugged. Great. No one had answers.

"He'll have to deal with his own people. He's Alpha. He has to be able to take charge if he wants to keep that position," Nova said.

"Date. Just go on dates with him," Emory said, looking off into space as she tried to picture the two of them alone, on a date, with no interference. What were the odds that that would ever happen in such a small town?

"Yeah. It could be romantic. I swear every time someone finds their mate, they just jump right into the sack and are suddenly living together. Oh, I just thought of another idea for a book," Nova said, grabbing her laptop and opening it.

Emory groaned, but Callie just winked at her with a smile. "It *could* be kind of romantic."

"Or it could be a total flop. I'm not exactly the romantic type." Such an understatement. She hadn't been with a man in so long, she wondered if everything still worked down there. And she'd never really, truly dated. What if she made a total fool of herself?

Nova was typing away when she glanced over the top of the laptop, her brows pulled together in concentration. "When was the last time you got laid?"

"Oh, hell no. You're not putting that in a book," Emory said, pushing to her feet.

She had so much to think about. She had to figure out how to approach Eli with the idea of dating. She had to figure out how to convince herself he wasn't Jace.

Emory waved at the girls over her shoulder and stepped out into the warm sun. Memories of her time with Jace threatened to buckle her knees, but just like she did every other time, she shoved that fucking memory as far back in her mind as possible and pretended that time of her life never happened.

She had a new life. She had a new family. And, if things went the way she hoped, she'd have a new mate soon.

****

Eli stared down at his phone, his heart in his fucking throat. Emory wanted to meet with him tonight. After the disaster at Moe's, he'd figured he wouldn't hear from her for a few days if at all.

Of course. When? Where? he typed back and hit send. He probably seemed eager as fuck, but he'd made his feelings known. There was no use trying to play it cool now.

He watched the conversation bubbles and waited impatiently. She wanted to try Moe's again. They'd have another audience. So this wasn't a date. This was probably her telling him to leave her alone. This was probably her telling him to fuck off.

Tossing his phone onto the coffee table, he flopped back onto the couch and threw his arm over his eyes.

"What now?" Luna asked from across the room.

His sister had an uncanny ability to sneak up on him no matter what he was doing. He pulled his arm away just enough to peek at her and growled softly. "Meeting Emory tonight," he said and put his arm back over his eyes.

"And you're mad about that?" she asked curiously.

He sat up and leaned forward, his elbows on his knees. "She wants to meet at Moe's. Last time we tried that, her entire Pack came."

"And you kissed her," she said with one brow raised.

Yeah. There had been that. He'd kissed dozens of women. But that had been the most erotic kiss of his life, and they'd barely done anything. The way his body reacted to her, he could only imagine how quickly he'd lose himself if he was ever able to bury himself to the hilt in her heat.

"You're overthinking it," Luna said, and turned to head up the stairs to his room she'd been using.

"What if she tells me to go away?" he asked, calling after her.

He felt a little panicked. He was excited to see her, but what the hell would he do if that was why she'd asked to meet with him? Could he control his lion? He barked out a short laugh. He could barely control him now. If Emory went away forever, his lion would end up getting Eli killed.

"Then you'll have to find a way to forget about her. Or you could continue to fight for her. But you'll respect her wishes." She shrugged. "I don't know what else to tell you."

That didn't help. Nothing his sister said put him at ease. He had three hours to dwell on every possibility of why Emory wanted to see him.

He was going to be a nervous wreck by the time he saw her face.

****

Emory checked her reflection one more time. She'd spent time doing her hair and makeup and found the cutest pair of jeans she owned and a top that made her boobs look good. Unfortunately, when it was time to go, her whole Pack was home.

"Where you going?" Reed asked as he and Micah climbed from his truck.

Tristan glared at her, but she ignored him.

"I have a date," Emory called back as she slung her purse over her shoulder, lifted her head high, and walked quickly to her car.

"With Eli," Gray said. He didn't ask and he didn't sound happy, either.

"Yep. I'll be home later. If one of you show up there tonight, I'll never forgive you," she said, stopping and turning to look at each of them before opening the car door.

"This isn't a good idea," Gray said.

Micah's arms were crossed over his chest and his eyes were a bright blue.

"You know what..." She could feel the anger welling inside of her. She hated to do it, but if the guys were going to be dicks, so was she. "I didn't say a word when Nova came here, did I? In fact, I'm pretty sure I was the first one to welcome her in. And when Callie got here, did I say a word about the trouble we'd have from the Pride? No," she said, turning her attention to Micah. "I welcomed her in and she became my sister. They both did. Now, all I'm asking is for the same fucking courtesy."

Nova and Callie were standing on Nova's porch, their heads bobbing up and down in agreement.

"Have fun and don't do anything I wouldn't do," Nova called out. Gray looked over his shoulder at her with an incredulous look. "What? She's right. She never made either of us feel like we didn't belong here, even though she could've. She's an adult. And...Emory, sorry about this, but," Nova said, glancing at Emory quickly before looking back at Gray, "Eli's her mate. Who the hell are any of you to tell her to stay away from him? You two, of all people, now how impossible that is." A wail came from inside. "Great. You made me wake Rieka up."

Nova threw her hands in the air and went inside to tend to her daughter.

The guys, except Tristan, looked a little confused and sheepish. They couldn't hold eye contact with Emory. Oh, but Tristan had no problem staring her down. He just stood there, a scowl imbedded on his handsome face, and shook his head slowly over and over again.

Well, whatever. He could be mad all he wanted. Yeah, she knew exactly why he was against this. He knew her past. But that was exactly what it was…her past. It was over and she refused to let it or her memories keep her from living her life. She refused to let bad shit that happened to her years ago keep her from finding happiness.

"I'll be home later. I'll text you if it gets late," Emory said. And then, just to be a little petty, she threw in, "Don't wait up," in a saccharine sweet voice and got into her car.

She might've seemed cool and pulled together at home, but now that she was on her way to see Eli, she was a big ball of nerves.

The drive to Moe's from her house took just under fifteen minutes. There were about a dozen cars and trucks parked out front, including Eli's blue Mustang. She'd always loved that car, but wondered why he didn't drive a truck like the guys from her Pack. Maybe he didn't have a job that required a work truck. Or maybe he just liked muscle cars.

And those were questions she'd learn the answer to, along with about a thousand others.

Grabbing the handle, she took three deep breaths before throwing her shoulders back and yanking the door open. A few people looked up to see who came in and went back to whatever they were doing, while the people she knew looked over her shoulder, no doubt waiting to see the rest of her Pack.

When they realized it was just her and she was moving directly toward Eli, a couple of them pulled their phones out. "They already know I'm here, jackasses," she yelled at Noah and Colton.

Colton at least looked apologetic. Noah, on the other hand, decided to glare at Eli.

She just ignored them and smiled at Eli when he stood as she came up to the table.

"Hi," she said, unsure of what to do or what to say. She wanted to hug him, peck a kiss to his cheek, something. Instead, she held her hand out like an idiot and shook his when he wrapped it around hers. His big hand dwarfed hers and that just made her think of other big things he possessed.

Yanking her hand back the second she realized where her mind was going, Emory nodded to his seat and sat down. He looked surprised when she took the one directly beside him instead of across from him as she'd done the day before.

"Hi," she said again, and then felt like the world's biggest dork.

There was a slight glisten to his forehead; he was sweating. Eli was as nervous as she was.

"You okay?" he asked, a tiny furrow to his brows.

"Yeah. Why wouldn't I be?"

"You said you needed to see me? What happened?"

Ohhh. He thought she needed something or was in trouble. She probably should've been a little clearer in her text. "Oh. Nothing happened. I literally just needed to see you," she said and then ducked her head when heat rushed her cheeks. Great. Now she was blushing.

Eli blinked a few times and then it was as if she saw the moment he'd caught on to what she was saying. His eyes went a little wide and a smile slowly spread across his adorable face.

"Nothing's wrong?" he asked.

"Nothing's wrong," she said.

"You just wanted to see me."

"Yeah," she said, ducking her gaze. Oh, come on. Since when was she shy? But it wasn't every day she found her mate and made up her mind to tell him she wanted to try to be with him.

"Wow," he breathed out.

"What?" she asked, frowning through a smile.

His eyes dropped to her lips then raised to her face. "I ran every scenario through my head but that one," he admitted.

"Why'd you think I wanted to see you?"

"To break up with me," he said, and then the cutest pink washed over his lightly whiskered cheeks.

She giggled, then closed her eyes when she realized the sounds she'd just made. Giggled? She'd seriously just giggled?

Clearing her throat in hopes of covering the sound, she wiped the smile off her face but kept her eyes soft. She had a few things to talk about before they ventured into this any further.

"Well, for one, you have to officially be together to break up," she said, trying and failing to hide her smile at the look on his face.

"You know what I meant," he said, his eyes dropping to his beer.

Seriously. They were both acting like teenagers on their first date. And you know what? She kind of liked it. It was exciting and heart warming and just…fun and easy.

"Gray doesn't want you in my Pack. I don't know if that'll change, but for now…stop stalking me every morning. Okay?"

"But—"

Emory held her hand up to stop him before he got any further. "I want to date," she blurted out before she lost her nerve.

"You want to date," he repeated. He had a habit of doing that.

"Yeah. I want to date, hang out with you, get to know each other better."

"You want to date," he said again, a smile spreading across that gorgeous face.

She lifted one shoulder. "Yeah. You know. Go out. Hang out. Tell each other our deepest, darkest…okay, maybe just tell each other our favorite colors and stuff."

"Turquoise," he said, leaning forward.

"What?"

"My favorite color is turquoise."

She tilted her head to the side and smiled with a confused frown. "That's an incredibly specific and odd favorite color."

"Your eyes are turquoise."

She blinked up at him, then that stupid heat rushed her neck and settled right in her cheeks. His favorite color was the color of her eyes. How romantic and mushy. Nova suddenly came to mind. Emory couldn't wait to tell Nova all about that one. She could definitely use it in one of her sappy books.

Pressing her hands to her cheeks, she tried to hide the blush while attempting to cool them.

"What's your favorite color?" he asked, that goofy smile still in place.

"Purple. But, like, grayish-purple."

He nodded like he was deep in thought or something. "Yeah. That fits you."

"How would you know?" she said.

As the minutes ticked by, she was growing more comfortable. Within the first twenty minutes, it no longer felt like a first date. It felt like they'd come here dozens of times, like they'd spent hundreds of hours talking.

"What about your family? You said you have a sister," Emory said, nodding at Noah as he brought two more beers and a menu. He just scowled down at her, glanced at Eli, and left.

"Yeah. Luna. She's my younger sister. She's still in the Pride. She and two other lionesses are living at my house until they figure something else out."

"How big is your house?" she asked. There was no way four people could easily stay inside her house or any of Big River Pack's houses.

"It's just a three-bedroom ranch." He opened the menu, then looked up when he realized she wasn't saying anything else. "What?"

"So, who's sharing your bed?"

He smiled. Then it faltered, but was back pretty quickly. "My sister. And she's not sharing it. She's sleeping in there by herself."

"So, who do you sleep with?" They weren't technically committed to each other, regardless of the mark on her neck, but the thought to him spooning up behind another female made her want to smash her bottle over his head.

She'd never been a violent person, but the urge to hurt someone was strong all of a sudden.

"No one, Em. I sleep on the couch. This is the first time any of them were able to live their life on their terms. They're not forced to stay with anyone they don't want to."

Emory watched Eli closely, watched for any tells, watched to see if he was bullshitting her. He held her gaze as if he could tell she was trying to see if he was lying to her.

"They're all free?" she asked with narrowed eyes.

"Every single one of them. Not all of them had it bad. Some of the guys were nice to their mates. But I gave the women the choice of whether they wanted to stay with the guys or not. Hence the reason I now have an estrogen overload in my house."

Three women in his home. He'd given up his bed. So, how would that work if they were able to make their relationship work? She'd already been fantasizing about being naked with him, but she had no desire to hump on a couch while there were three other people in the house who could walk in on them any time.

Pushing that question to the end of the long line of questions, she opened her own menu and scanned it. She knew the selection of food. They'd been to Moe's enough times she practically had it memorized. But she needed to hide her face for a second and give her hands something to do other than fidget.

Eli took the order up to Noah instead of waiting for him to make his rounds again. Emory didn't bother hiding the fact she was checking him out. She'd already told her Pack he was her mate. She'd already told them she was going on a date with Eli.

And he was one fine piece of man. If she wanted to check him out, that was her business. She winked at Colton when he smirked and shook his head, but at least he wasn't shooting her disgruntled looks or glaring at Eli like Noah and Luke were. He seemed curious and kind of happy for Emory.

For some reason, Colton's reluctant acceptance of Emory and Eli's union meant the most to her. If anyone had the right to hold a grudge, it was Colton. It had been his dad who'd been murdered by the former Alpha of Tammen. It had been his dad who'd been slaughtered by a lion.

If he didn't hold it against Eli, then neither should anyone else.

Eli stopped at a table and said something to a group of guys. She recognized them. They were Tammen lions. They looked up at her when Eli pointed and smiled. They made eye contact with Emory and dipped their heads once, a show of respect.

That, she hadn't expected. For some reason, she'd expected leering or even sneering. Not a quick hello and then back to business. They didn't stare at her, even as Eli walked away and back to her. They didn't point and whisper.

"What did you tell them?" she asked Eli when he sat back down so close his thigh was pressed against hers.

"I told them I was on a date with my mate," he said, his hand disappearing under the table to land on her knee.

Emory started, but relaxed when he began to pull it away. It was odd. The moment his hand was away from her, her knee felt cold and empty. And she'd officially become a character in one of Nova's freaking books.

"I don't mind," she said, reaching for his hand and putting it back on her knee. "You just scared me."

Instead of keeping his hand there, he turned it over and thread his fingers through hers. It felt so natural. It felt so good.

Were they moving too fast? No. They hadn't done anything yet, short of a little petting. Hell. They were in public and surrounded by their friends, not like there was much they could do there.

If they were alone…yeah, she was pretty sure she'd have a hell of a time keeping her hands off him. Even with the way he was looking at her now, like he was waiting for her to say something profound, she couldn't help but admire the cut of his jaw, the dark stubble on his cheeks, the small dimple in his chin, the way his eyes had gold flecks in the brown irises. He was ruggedly beautiful.

"You're so hot," she said, and didn't have an ounce of regret for saying it.

His smile widened and he leaned forward a little. "You're beautiful," he said, his face so close to hers.

She wanted him to close the space between them and let her taste his lips. But they had an audience. She didn't even have to look up to know they were being watched closely and every move was being reported back to Gray or Reed.

"What made you change your mind?" he asked, inhaling deeply like he was breathing her in and leaning back a little.

"About us?"

"Yeah."

She lifted one shoulder again. "I don't know. Why shouldn't we be happy, too? And Nova mentioned something about Romeo and Juliet." She'd brought them up because of his tendency of hiding in the woods and watching her house, but she'd just thought about the fact they were from two feuding families.

"They were kids and lived for three days after causing a bunch of deaths," he said, his brows causing a slight crease.

"That's what I said!" she said a little too loud. "What I mean, though, was even with everything standing in their way, and the fact they were from two families that hated each other, they were willing to do anything they had to to make their love work."

"Love," he said, his voice deeper. Ooooh, she really liked his voice all deep and husky like that.

"Well, yeah. They thought they were in love. I mean, who knows. They were thirteen and seventeen and—" All thoughts and words were cut off by his lips against hers.

He just stayed like that, his mouth slanted over hers. He didn't try to dip his tongue in her mouth. He didn't tangle his fingers in her hair, although she totally wanted him to. Just kissed her and fed her so much passion.

When Eli pulled away, his face inches from hers, his gold eyes staring down into hers, she struggled to catch her breath. What was it about him that always made her body feel like she'd been running a marathon?

"Sorry. I've wanted to do that since you sat down," he admitted. His eyes were roaming her face, dipping from her eyes, to her nose, to her mouth, then back like he was committing her to memory.

She knew the feeling. She couldn't quite keep her eyes from him, either.

Before long, people were finishing up their drinks, paying their tabs, and leaving. Yet, Emory and Eli hadn't run out of conversation.

They talked about favorite foods–he liked fish, which she hated. They talked about favorite music–they both loved outlaw country and alternative. They talked about movies–he hated musicals, one of her faves. They had a lot in common in some areas and none in others. Where they disagreed in tastes, though, they seemed to complement each other.

It was just a normal first date, even if she was ready to take him out to the car and suck face. Then again, maybe that was normal for a first date. She didn't have much to compare it with.

"It's getting late," she said, reluctantly glancing up at Noah who was once again watching them closely.

"Yeah. I'm surprised your Pack hasn't already come looking for you," Eli said.

She stood and grabbed her bag from the back of her chair. "They know better this time," she said. "And who are you to talk. I notice your guys are still here." She jabbed her thumb over her shoulder at the Tammen guys who were pretending not to watch their every move.

He shrugged. "I'm their Alpha. You're a member of Big River. They're just being protective."

She snorted. Eli was big. Not quite as big as Colton or the other Blackwater guys, but he could definitely take care of himself. "Pretty sure you don't need protecting."

He walked her out, clapping one of his guys on the shoulder as he passed, and stopped beside her car.

"We're really going to do this?" he asked, his brows high, excitement in his pretty eyes.

She leaned against the side of her car and arched her neck back to look up at him. He was so tall. And she was so short. How silly they must look together. Or cute. Yeah, she was going with cute.

"Yeah. We're really going to try," she said, her eyes dipping to his lips like they had a mind of their own. She desperately wanted him to kiss her goodnight. A real kiss this time.

He stepped into her space and cupped her face, his fingers grazing the side of her neck as his thumb gently caressed her cheek. His hand was so warm, rough and calloused, yet soft and gentle.

There was still this part of her that wanted to hate him for marking her. To hold onto that anger of having the choice taken from her.

But had there been any choice other than him?

She'd never felt this excited about a male. She'd never felt an ounce of this same passion with Jace. She'd never wondered what kind of future they could have or thought of ways to make him smile. With Jace, it had all been forced. It was what she had to do to survive.

With Eli, however, she couldn't wait to see how he liked his eggs in the morning. She couldn't wait to find out what kind of sounds he made when they made love. She couldn't wait to find out how he'd look when the gray started to creep into his dark hair and lines appeared around his eyes.

She realized it wasn't just now she was excited about. It wasn't just the lust building inside of her that had her looking forward to getting to know Eli better. It was a deep-rooted bond they'd formed before they'd ever spoken a single word to each other.

Maybe his lion and her wolf had chosen for them, but, damn, she was glad her animal had chosen him.

Chapter Four

The smile on Emory's face just wouldn't fade. That had gone better than she could've hoped. There were a few times when the door opened when she thought her Pack was coming to interrupt their date. But they'd never shown.

It had just been Eli and Emory. Well, and a bar full of people they knew. Yet, not one person gave them any more trouble than a few scowls and glares. And, honestly, she'd been paying too much attention to Eli that she'd barely noticed the looks.

He'd kissed her. He'd for real kissed her.

His hands had been so warm as he cupped her face and leaned in, moving so slowly as if giving her plenty of time to decide if she wanted to put the brakes on the whole thing. Not a chance would that have happened. She'd been dying to kiss him all night, more than just the sweet press of lips they'd had inside.

Eli's mouth tasted like beer and something sweet, something all him. And wowza, could he kiss. She swore her toes had curled inside her shoes.

She chuckled as she thought about telling Nova and Callie in the morning. Nova called the big O the toe curler. If Eli had made her feel like she was feverish with just a kiss, she could only imagine how badly she'd combust when they were naked and skin to skin.

Her phone dinged in the console. Grabbing it, she used her voice command and asked Siri to read her last text.

A feminine, robotic voice filled the quiet of her car. "Had a great time. Can't wait to see you again. Text me when you're home safe."

Sweet. And considerate.

Her phone dinged again. Once again, she asked Siri for her assistance.

"Tell Gray I said hey."

Sweet, considerate, and a total smartass. If her family would just give him a chance, they'd realize how much like them he really was.

He made her laugh as hard as Reed did, was as intense as Micah at times, strong and loyal like Gray, and even had a mysterious side like Tristan. It was like Eli was all her favorite guys rolled into one.

"Shit," she whispered. She'd actually forgotten to ask him what he did for a living. They'd talked about everything, just constantly fired questions at each other and laughed so much, it had completely slipped her mind. The lions had to work to afford their muscle cars and the homes they all lived in.

Whatever he did, she couldn't picture him behind a desk. And his human eye color still wasn't very human. There was way too much gold to pass as human enough to work in an office. And he had to have cultivated those delicious muscles from somewhere.

"Siri, text Eli," she called out. The second she heard the telltale beep, she said, "Had fun. Text me tomorrow."

There was so much more she wanted to say. She wanted to tell him how much she'd enjoyed his company, how sexy that kiss had been, how good his chest had felt under her palms. But that was way too much for a quick text.

Her phone dinged as she pulled up the long driveway and she took the second to glance down and then frowned. **I don't understand.**

She reread what Siri had sent: **A ton. Sexy sorry.**

"What the fuck, Siri," she said, her face getting hot. She read out loud as she texted the second her car was parked alongside everyone else's vehicles. "Had. Fun. Text me tomorrow," she said, enunciating every word. He probably thought she was an idiot.

He sent back an emoji laughing with tears. Okay. He realized she'd been a victim to Siri's legendary text sabotage.

With the biggest, goofiest smile on her face, she yanked her purse from the passenger seat, closed her car door as quietly as possible so she wouldn't wake Rieka - or anyone else - and was damn near skipping to her door.

"You're late," Tristan said, scaring the shit out of her as she took the first stair up her porch.

"Why the hell are you sneaking around in the shadows?" she whisper-screamed at him, her hand against her chest to keep her heart from bursting through her rib cage.

"Not a good idea," he said, stepping around her porch and coming close enough for her to make out his features.

His eyes were bright blue and his brows were knitted together. He crossed his arms over his chest, and the sweet guy who'd been her confidant and companion for a few years before they'd found Big River looked almost intimidating. He definitely looked pissed.

"Remember Jace?" he said, raising one brow before going right back to frowning.

"Of course I remember. I was there. It's not the same."

She turned her back on him to go inside, but his hand clamped around her wrist and pulled her back to him.

"Too dangerous, Em. Not a wolf."

"Neither is Callie."

"A fucking lion."

"So is Callie."

"Not the same. You know that."

This was the most she'd heard him say at once in a long time. Her Pack would shit themselves if they heard him using almost full sentences. Hell, they'd shit themselves if they heard him actually not only starting the conversation, but continuing it. She knew the strain was going to be too much soon, but he was the one who'd come to her. If he was growing uncomfortable with each word, then he could just keep them to himself and let her live her own life.

"Tristan," she said, then took a deep breath and tried to calm her anger. She knew Tristan loved her like a sister. He'd looked out for her just like she had for him. He'd been her rock while she'd been his voice for years.

But here, with their new Pack, with them both being different people, they could just be themselves. Why he still hid his disability from Gray and the rest of Big River so many years later was a mystery to her.

"Look, I know you're worried about me. I promise I'm okay. Eli isn't Jace. It's just not the same. Yeah, he's a lion, but he's a good guy. You know I'm a better judge of character than that." Again, with that raised eyebrow. "Okay, I'm a better judge *now*. How about this?

If he does anything to hurt me, you get to kick his ass. Does that make you feel better?"

He snorted but didn't smile. He dropped his head and kicked a rock with his bare toe. He was wearing nothing but a pair of boxer briefs, which meant he was in bed when he heard her pull in and had rushed out here.

"No. Be careful," he said, shoved her shoulder, and headed back to his own little house.

"Love you," she called to him quietly.

"Same," he said, then disappeared inside.

Emory tilted her head back and stared at the sky full of bright twinkling stars. Ever since she'd met Eli, everything seemed just a little brighter, a little more colorful...

And a crap load more terrifying.

Even her sappy, love sick thoughts freaked her out. She'd never been so into a guy that she was willing to piss off the people she cared most about just to be with him. She was willing to gamble on a possible forever when she still really knew nothing about him.

Damn. She really hoped this didn't turn into a modern-day Romeo and Juliet, because she'd never forgive herself if someone other than herself got hurt.

****

Eli sat in his car and just stared at Emory's text. That had been the best date of his entire life. And he knew it was because of who he was on a date with. She'd been charming and sexy and fun. She'd still given him sass and attitude, but that was just part of the aforementioned charm. He didn't know what he'd do if she all of a sudden turned into some sweet, submissive girl. He liked it when she gave him shit. He liked it when she busted his balls. He liked her warped and sometimes morbid sense of humor.

But even though she'd seemed comfortable with him, he couldn't help but feel a small amount of fear radiating from her. He just hoped it wasn't fear of him.

She definitely didn't exhibit any fear when he'd gotten the courage to really kiss her. Sure, he'd given her somewhat of a peck inside, but that was just because he couldn't hold back anymore. As soon as she started talking about love, something inside of him kind of snapped and he went for it. And she was into it.

And then? And then he'd kissed her for real. Her small hands had gripped his shirt at his waist at first before finally smoothing up his stomach to rest on his pecs. He could've kissed her all night, but he needed her to set the pace. When she pulled back, he fought every instinct to chase her mouth. He needed to hear that soft moan she'd emitted when their tongues touched again.

His dick thumped against his zipper as he thought about her body pressed up against his, about her hands roaming his chest, the way her lips had molded around his. His heart and animal were begging for more of her, but so was his fucking body.

But it would all be on her time. If she needed him to wait, he'd wait as long as she needed. He might go blind from jerking off, but he'd fucking wait.

There was only one light on inside his house and that was his bedroom. Luna had waited up for him. And for once, he was excited to tell her everything.

Jumping from his car, he hurried through the front door and jogged up the stairs taking them two at a time. Luna was sitting up in bed, the blankets over her legs, a book open in her hands. Her eyes immediately rose to him when he stepped through the door.

With a smile, she set her book down on her lap. "I take it from the twinkle in your eye the night went well."

"Oh yeah," he said, his breath coming in pants.

"So, she didn't ask you there to give you bad news?" she asked, cocking one blonde brow at him.

"Nope. She wants to try dating. She wants to see where this goes. And I kissed her…twice."

"Nice," she said with a soft chuckle. "Her Pack show up again?"

"Nope. The Blackwater and a few Ravenwood guys were there, but they all left us alone."

"No one said anything?"

"Nope. They shot me some dirty looks, but I don't give a fuck about that. She didn't notice or didn't care, so I don't either."

His heart was pitter pattering in his chest. He pressed the palm of his hand against his sternum and made little circles. "She's so fucking beautiful," he breathed out, almost as if he were talking to himself. "And sexy as hell. And so fucking funny."

"You're so cheesy," she teased, picking her book back up and looking at the page. "When are you going to see her again?" she asked.

Fuck. He wanted to see her again right then, but he didn't want to seem pushy. "Is it true you girls don't like for guys to text you the next day after a date?" he asked. He'd much rather call her. He was dying to hear her voice before going to bed.

"No. That's such bullshit. I think a guy made that up. I mean, don't be all clingy or whatever, but you can text her tomorrow. Just don't send her a three-page love poem."

"Yeah, because I'm super poetic."

He turned to leave, his hand on the doorknob, but looked back at Luna. "You want to meet her?"

She set her book back on her lap and tilted her head at him. He knew it was a long shot. Luna rarely left the territory, and always wore long sleeved shirts and a bunch of makeup to cover her scars. Getting her into Moe's or somewhere else equally public would be a struggle.

"Someday," she said after a few seconds of a stare down.

Well, that was better than hell no. Maybe she was finally coming around. He knew the outside world made her nervous, but it was full of some really great people. Yeah, some of them were assholes, but they were outnumbered. At least in his experience.

Then again, most people gave him a wide berth whenever they were in his proximity. Even humans with their dull senses could tell they were in the presence of a predator. And his size, tattoos, and oddly colored eyes didn't help.

Eli waved over his shoulder as he pulled the door shut after Luna dismissed him with a smirk and "goodnight." He knew he'd be awake for a while. He was full of restless energy and so excited about the way the night had gone. He'd been fully prepared to have his heart crushed. He'd been ready to lose the fight with his lion and end up getting taken out by his entire Pride.

Emory might never know, but she'd saved his life. No. She'd never know because he'd never tell her. That was too much for anyone to have to carry.

She didn't know she carried his sanity and entire life in those tiny little hands of hers. And if he were real honest with himself, she'd been carrying his heart for months.

****

Emory had to work that day, but she really wanted to stay home and gossip with the girls. Instead, she'd have to either hold it in until later or talk with the guys listening. She couldn't wait to tell them everything, about how much fun she'd had, about how funny Eli was, about how sexy that damn kiss was.

She was still obsessed with how his body had felt under her hands. If she'd let her fingers do whatever the hell they'd wanted, they would've ended up skimming past his belt and made a beeline south. Not yet. She wanted to do everything one could do without clothes with him, but not yet. She'd been pushed into something too quickly when she was younger and it had turned into a disaster. She was older and wiser now and would protect her body and heart and would pace herself.

At least she'd try really hard to pace herself.

Her cheeks were warm as she stepped into the feed store and smiled at every coworker and customer she passed. Was this what falling in love was like? Or did everyone go through this giddy emotional rollercoaster when they met someone new?

Either way, she was quite enjoying the feeling.

The day went faster than she'd thought it would when all she wanted to do was leave. She'd received one text from Eli that morning, just a simple one wishing her a great day and telling her he'd dreamed of her. Yeah, she knew the feeling. She'd had all kinds of naughty dreams about the big Shifter last night.

One eye on the clock, Emory finished up her shift, sent Eli a text that she was heading home, then hurried out the door. Nova and Callie would already be there since neither of them had jobs. But the guys would be home soon, too. She wanted to get out as much as possible before she had an audience of growling, sneering men.

Both of her friends were sitting around the cold fire pit when she pulled up, little Rieka in a playpen beside them. Emory bent over to kiss the baby, then plopped down in a chair beside Nova, dropping her purse onto the ground.

"Girls!" she said, that same perma-smile in place.

"Oh lord. I take it the night went well?" Nova said. She pulled a can of soda from the cooler under her feet and handed it to Emory.

"The man can kiss," Emory said.

"And what other things can he do well?" Nova said with one brow raised.

"Oh my god, Nova. It was our first date. That's all we did."

"All night long?" Nova asked as she winked at Callie.

Callie smiled, but it seemed forced.

"What's up? Why do you look not look happy with my news?" Emory asked, popping the tab on her Pepsi.

"Where were you guys? Were you in public?" Callie asked, lifting her hand and chewing on the skin around her thumb nail.

"Yeah. I told you guys we were going to Moe's. Just about everyone was there. About as public as it gets."

"Were there any Tammen guys there?" Callie asked, her brows furrowing a quick second before her face went neutral again.

Emory looked from Callie to Nova then back again. "Yeah. Two of them that I know of. Why does that matter?"

Callie's shoulders raised in a sort of half shrug. "Did he kind of…parade you around?"

Emory's head snapped back. "Uh, no. We sat at a table toward the back of the room all night. Alone."

Callie's brows shot up. "He didn't introduce you at all?"

"No. I mean, when he went up to the bar he stopped and talked to them for a second and pointed me out, but that was it. What are you getting at, Callie?"

"Male lions like to show off their newest female," she said bluntly.

"Well, he didn't show me off. And I'm not technically his."

"Actually, you kind of are. But now that the laws have changed, you actually get the choice," Callie corrected Emory.

Right. She technically was his because of the claiming mark on the back of her neck.

"Whatever. I haven't marked him."

"You don't have to. Remember? He's a lion. Females don't mark their mates," Callie said before going back to chewing the skin around her thumb.

Callie's questions and her nervous habit were making Emory anxious. Eli had told her he'd told his Tammen guys who she was and that she was his mate. That wasn't exactly showing her off or parading her around. But what if he'd said more? She couldn't see him being that kind of guy, but like she kept reminding herself, she really didn't know much about him other than some superficial facts.

Her mood was quickly falling and all because of a few seeds of doubt planted by Callie's time with Tammen. If anyone knew the habits of male lions, it would be her. She was supportive of Emory's choices, but she was telling her to be careful in her own way instead of demanding she stay away like Tristan.

"You don't think he's trying to trick me or something, do you?" she asked Callie after a few minutes of stewing.

"If he was doing that, why would he support the new laws, Em? He's a good guy," Nova said, frowning at Callie. She already had the mom look down.

He was a good guy. As far as Emory could tell. But even good guys had needs. And Shifter needs weren't like that of humans. They still had a human side, sure, but they were also led by their more primal side. Their animal was who picked their real mates. It was their animal who came out more often when someone they cared about was in trouble. It was their animal side who tended to behave in a possessive manner.

Emory didn't really know much about Eli's lion. But, again, she didn't really know much about Eli the man, either.

That's why we're dating, she silently reminded herself. She was trying to get to know him so she didn't make a stupid, life changing decision.

Leaning back in her chair, she propped her elbows on the rests and massaged her temples with the pads of her fingers. She'd been so high on the night before, she hadn't bothered thinking about anything else.

Now, she was back to wondering where exactly they'd live if they did work out. How would his Pride treat her after everything their two groups had gone through? Would the women welcome her in or see her as a threat? Would the guys treat her as an equal, or see her as a potential baby maker?

And could Eli really live with the fact she would never change her mind about motherhood?

"What's going through your pretty little head?" Nova asked.

"Everything," she said with a huff of frustration. Why couldn't she have held on to the good feelings for a little while longer? Now all her doubts were racing back, each one fighting for attention in her brain. "Back to doubting everything."

"Why?" Nova asked, her eyes shooting over to Callie.

"I'm sorry. I shouldn't have said anything," Callie said. "It's just...well, you're my sister now. Isn't that what sisters do? Aren't we supposed to worry about each other and never like each other's boyfriends or whatever?"

"Does that mean I can rip on Micah now?" Nova asked, one brow cocked.

Callie snorted. "You know what I mean. I just don't want you to get hurt, Em. I know you're smart. You won't let him manipulate you."

Emory really didn't think that was what he was doing, though. She was the one who'd asked to see him. She'd picked the place and time and tone of the date. And he'd been respectful and sweet and sexy.

Always back to the sexy. For some reason, her body found the need to remind her brain how sexy Eli really was.

He wasn't someone she would've gone for in the past. He was so inked up. She couldn't help but think about how much of his body was covered in tats. His hair was a little longer than she normally liked and kind of messy in an intentional way. Oh, and there was that little thing of him being a freaking lion.

"Ugh!" she groaned out and dropped her head back against the rest. "What the hell do I do?"

"About what?" Nova asked.

"What do you mean, about what? Have you not been following along? About Eli," Emory said, frowning over at Nova.

"Thought you already decided to give him a shot."

"Yeah. That was until Callie reminded me that he was not only a lion but a Tammen fucking lion."

"Callie's a lion and it worked out fine."

"And she's a female. Not to mention, she and Micah built a relationship before he bit her."

"Actually…" Callie said, smiling sheepishly. "We were still pretty new when he marked me."

"But did you want him to?" Emory asked.

"Well, yeah."

"So did you," Nova said. When Emory shot her a glare, Nova raised both hands. "You can give me the poo poo eye all you want, but we all saw the way you two watched each other. I knew something was going to happen before you did."

"Oh, bullshit," Emory said, pushing to her feet and scooping her bag from the ground.

"Yep. You two were practically shooting arrows at each other from your eyes. And not those flaming kinds from old wars. The kinds with hearts attached to the front."

"Did you just refer to us as Cupids?" Emory asked, tugging her bag over her shoulder.

"Sure. Whatever. What I'm saying is, you two were mated before you were mated."

"And, as usual, you make very little sense." Emory just stood there with her arms crossed over her chest, her bag hanging at her side, but didn't go inside her house. She wanted to be alone but didn't. She needed the support of her friends, but needed to think. Stupid confused brain.

"Listen, you said you wanted to date him. You date to get to know each other. Give him a chance before you decide to write him off and make yourself miserable."

"How do you figure I'd be miserable?"

"Uh, because you came floating over here to brag about Eli's tongue kiss abilities? Because you didn't stop smiling until Callie Kitty brought up the whole lion thing? Because you still haven't stormed off to pout? You want him. So have him. And if the time comes where you think it's time to bail, then move on. Although…"

"Although, what, Nova?"

"We both know carrying someone's mark doesn't mean shit. All those lionesses were marked. But I can smell the difference in your blood. That was a true mate bite. Your animals have already chosen. No matter what happens, you two are bonded for life."

Emory dropped her head with another frustrated groan. She'd already thought about all that. When Eli had promised to stay away from her, there was a part of her that wanted to beg him to take her away and make love to her. There was a part of her that wanted to beg him to stay at her side. But, like Tristan made sure to remind her, she'd had a mate before. And that had turned into nothing short of a nightmare.

"Are you going to see him again tonight?" Callie asked. She did one of those apologetic smiles with her brows pulled up and together. "I didn't mean to make you doubt him."

"I already doubted the whole thing. I'm just tired of…fuck…I'm kind of tired of being alone. And if you tell anyone what I'm about to say, I'll freeze every single bra you own."

Nova and Callie both held up their hands, fingers together, like they were Boy Scouts making a pledge.

"I'm tired of being alone, I hate being away from him, and my freaking wolf goes nuts the second I'm not texting him or talking to him or able to see his face. She's never been this crazy in my head, but now she's like one of those clingy girlfriends from the movies."

"You're falling in love," Nova said, her voice all dreamy.

"I am not."

"Me thinks thou doth protest too much," Nova said.

"You're ridiculous," Emory said and turned to head inside. But she didn't bother hiding the smile since her back was to Nova.

Okay, so she was protesting. A lot. But she was trying to be careful while attempting to allow herself to feel for a man. The thought of fully allowing him or anyone for that matter into her life and heart scared the crap out of her. She'd spent the last five years learning how to be herself again. She'd struggled to come back after the disaster that was her life with Jace.

She hadn't bothered mentioning her ex to Eli. And, honestly, she wasn't sure if she should. Or could. It was hard enough when Tristan brought it up. At least her wolf was no longer punishing her for her lack of judgement. To her defense, she'd been young and hadn't been given much of a choice.

Memories of her blue-eyed, blond-haired former mate crashed into her the second she was alone. Why now? She'd found happiness, even if just for a few hours, so why did Jace have to haunt her now?

Eli was Jace's complete opposite in almost every way. Where Jace was blond, Eli was black-haired. Where Jace was bare of any marks, including scars, Eli was covered in art and had silver lines cutting through the dark lines. Where Jace had never seen a minute of manual labor, Eli's hands were calloused and strong.

Maybe that was why her wolf had chosen Eli; he was as far removed from Jace as a man could be. Except one thing...

They were both lions.

Jace had been the one and only man she'd ever been tied to outside her species, and look how that had gone.

Tossing her bag onto the counter, she stripped as she made her way to the bathroom. She threw her clothes in the washing machine immediately; just leaving a shirt on the floor made her tiny house seem cluttered.

She needed a shower. She needed to wash off not only the day, but the memories that were threatening to drown her. And she needed to wash away her doubt and trepidation and remind herself Eli wasn't Jace. Eli wasn't Rhett. He was her mate, the male her animal had chosen, the man her heart had chosen.

You're falling in love, Nova's voice whispered in her head as she soaped up and stood under the hot spray.

Love? She wasn't sure about all that. She really couldn't say she'd ever loved anyone, outside of her own Pack and a few friends. But romantic love was a whole different beast. Nope. She'd never felt the kind of thing Nova described in all her romance books.

Oh, but she wanted to. She desperately wanted to feel that way about Eli. She just didn't know if her heart and brain would ever agree on anything. Her heart knew exactly what it wanted. It was her brain giving her all the fits. It was her brain that reminded her that maybe she wasn't worthy of finding what Micah and Gray had. It was her brain that reminded her that maybe Jace was all she'd ever get. It was her brain that reminded her that there still was that whole *where would they live thing* hanging between her and Eli.

She hadn't even brought that up last night. And neither had he. They'd just talked and laughed and teased for hours. The night had flown by far too quickly. And then it was time to go and her wolf whined in her head until she finally fell into a fitful sleep.

Fitful might have been a little much to describe a night filled with vivid sex dreams. But it still kept her from getting a full eight hours.

With a towel wrapped around her body, she leaned against the sink and stared at her reflection. Did Eli even think about the fact she was a wolf? Did it matter to him? He didn't appear to be scared of her Pack, but that didn't mean he respected them, either.

That was a total lie. Why else would he have come to warn them that Rhett was planning something months ago? He'd tried to warn them before anything happened and had kept Emory safe. Even if he didn't like Gray or the other guys, it was obvious there was some form of respect there.

Emory dried off with a little more vigor than was necessary and her skin was pink by the time she was done. Why couldn't this be easy like it was for Micah and Gray?

She stopped mid-scrub and huffed out a laugh.

Who was she fooling? There had been nothing easy about the relationships between her Alpha and Second and their mates. They'd been rife with threats and violence from the start. Both females had run to Big River for protection. It was fate that had paired them up the way they had.

Fate or not, Nova was right; their stories sure did make for great books. She'd done fairly well with both new books, although she'd finally stopped writing about Shifters. In her new books, the heroes–and sometimes heroines–were vampires or witches. Nova refused to leave the paranormal romance world for what she referred to as too much reality for her taste.

Was Emory meeting Eli purely fate, as well? Of all the men who could've chased after Callie, it was Eli. It just happened to be the one male her wolf noticed after so many years. She'd been attracted to guys, sure, but she'd never felt so connected to another person as she did with Eli.

Her animal would never choose a bad guy. She had to believe that. And, if she ever got the nerve to finally visit his territory, she had to believe both he and his lion would keep her safe from any holdovers of the former law. There might be some there who believed that since he'd marked her, he owned her.

Did her not immediately moving in with him show weakness to his Pride?

That was his business. It was up to him to keep his Pride under control. It was up to him to lead them and show them how things should be.

Instead of getting dressed, she padded across the room in her towel and lowered onto her folded-up futon. She'd always been adamant about folding her blankets and tucking her futon away every day, and that morning had been no exception. Micah and Reed would just plop their dirty bodies down on the sheets and blankets where they slept. Or, at least, Micah used to before Callie came along.

Emory needed a tidy space or she got nervous. What was Eli's room like? What was his house like? Did he keep it clean? Or did he expect the women now residing in his home to keep it up, like his own live-in housekeepers?

That thought ruffled her feathers a little. She liked her house clean, but she wouldn't be the only one to keep up on everything. Any guy she finally allowed into her space would have to pick up after himself. She didn't want to be a mother and that included mothering her mate.

Sitting straight up on the futon, she realized she was picturing Eli in her space. She was picturing his belongings mingled in with her own. He probably had way too much stuff to fit in with hers since he'd been living in a larger house for so long, but she was still imagining his shoes sitting beside hers at the front door, a second towel hanging over the rack drying after his shower, his clothes folded neatly beside hers in the drawers she'd built in under the loft stairs.

He was Alpha of Tammen; could he leave his Pride and stay in Big River with her? Not could he…*would* he? Would he be willing to give up his Pride to live with her there?

And, more importantly, could she ever ask him to do that? Was she so afraid to live among the lions that she'd ask him to abandon his own people, his own freaking sister, to be with her?

"This sucks," she moaned out as she dropped her head back against the cushion.

Had Micah and Gray gone through so much inner turmoil when they'd found their mates? Being as both women had run to their territory, probably not.

Emory stared at her phone sitting on the small table beside the futon. She wanted to see him. She was terrified to see him. She had so many questions, yet was scared of the answers.

Her wolf began to pace and whine in her head and made her decision for her.

She grabbed her phone and typed out a text to Eli. **Hang out tonight?** Send.

Not the most romantic invitation, but her brain was too all over the place to try for much more than that.

Name the place and time, his text read after three seconds.

She smiled at the screen, even gently swiped her thumb over his words. He was just as eager to see her as she was him.

The question now was where? They could go back to Moe's and be in public again. Callie seemed to feel really strongly about that. Or they could find somewhere a little quieter and actually get to know each other without all the glares and stares.

Did she really care about the looks, though? Did she really care what others thought of what she was doing or how she was living her life? While her Pack didn't like it, they were giving her enough distance to explore this mate thing with Eli, so why couldn't Noah and the others?

Emory tried to imagine the two of them somewhere quiet and private. And then she pictured herself climbing onto his lap and shoving her tongue down his throat.

No. They needed to be in public, at least for now. She didn't need the risk of not only making a fool of herself, but moving them too fast.

Moe's it was. She replied, telling him to meet her at seven. That would give her enough time to find something cute to wear, do her hair and makeup, and prep her Pack for another night with Eli.

Trucks rumbled up the driveway as she realized she'd have to once again warn them away from crashing her date.

Her phone dinged as she watched the trucks come into view and kick dust up from the driveway. **Invite your Pack**, Eli texted.

What? No way. Last time they showed up, everything went to shit.

Then again, when they'd crashed her meeting with Eli, everything was different. She'd made up her mind to stay away from him, that she was just going to keep his lion at bay. Things were *way* different now. If Eli was going to be in her life, she needed to make sure the Pack was at least partially on board.

But this was only their second date. Third if she counted the first failure of a meeting. Shouldn't they spend more time getting to know each other before he got thrown in front of the firing squad? Because she knew the second anyone had the chance, they'd pepper him with questions about his Pride, about his family, and about his intentions with Emory.

Dressing quickly, she ran over to Callie's and knocked on her door like a crazy woman until Callie pulled it open with a look of concern on her pretty face.

"What? What happened?" Her eyes rose over Emory's head to her mate riding in Reed's truck. "Is it Micah?"

"What?" Emory glanced over her shoulder then back at Callie. "Oh. No. Sorry. Didn't mean to freak you out. I've got to talk to you real fast before they get out. Eli wants me to invite the whole Pack out on our date tonight," she rushed out as quickly as she could, glancing over her shoulder in a panic as the guys stepped from their trucks.

Micah's eyes were narrowed on where Emory was standing on his and Callie's porch.

Emory forced a smile at Micah and turned back to Callie. "Hurry. What should I do?"

"Only invite Gray and Nova," she whispered quickly. "Not the whole Pack. Not yet. That's too much and Micah will just glare and growl and Reed will make inappropriate jokes and be a fool. Tristan…well, Tristan will probably just sit there and stew silently."

They both snorted softly as Tristan climbed from his truck and frowned at them. There was no way the guys didn't know Emory and Callie were conspiring, but it was none of their business. For now, anyway.

"Okay. Good plan. Thanks."

She turned, took a step down, turned back, and hugged Callie around the shoulders. "I'll be careful," she promised on a whisper.

Callie hugged her back and let her go, waving as she stepped off her porch. "Have fun and tell me everything tomorrow."

Well, maybe not everything. Callie had acted a little too nervous for Emory's taste when she'd come bouncing over with her news after work. Nova was the one who was always good for some extra *oohing* and *ahhing* when it came to romance stories.

Emory jogged bare foot back to her house, ran through the door, and scooped her phone back up. She sent Eli a text that she'd only invite Nova and Gray. He just sent back **K**.

She hated that reply from anyone. It was apathetic at best and hard to interpret. Was he hurt that she wasn't inviting everyone? Pissed? Or was he busy and that was the best he had time to send?

Emory decided to get ready before she went to talk to Nova and Gray. That way, if they said no, she could just slink away and be ready for her date, instead of sulking and being pissed that her Alpha had rejected her invitation.

She took a little extra time on her makeup, smoking her eyes out the way Nova had shown her, and applied two coats of mascara. Nova was right; it made her eyes look so big and bright with it done like this. She kept her lips pretty bare, just swiping on a coat of lip gloss. If the night ended the way it did last night, she didn't want to leave lipstick smeared all over both of their faces.

And boy, did she really hope for another kiss. As long as Nova and Gray left before she did. She'd have to make sure she drove herself so she'd have a little private time to tell her mate goodnight before heading home.

Her wardrobe left a lot to be desired, but she'd never been one for trends. That was all Nova's wheel house. Where Nova loved her cute boots and sandals and her skinny jeans, Emory had six pairs of the exact same style and color of jeans. She just grabbed a pair and a t-shirt that hugged her boobs nicely. After all, that seemed to be where Eli's eyes drifted when he thought she didn't notice. He was definitely a boob man.

Grabbing her favorite pair of boots, she slipped her feet in, then ran over to Gray's.

Nova, thankfully, was the one who opened the door. "You think your dad can babysit tonight? Or Callie and Micah? Or Reed?"

"Reed can not babysit tonight," Reed yelled from his porch.

"Or not Reed," Emory said, frowning over at him.

"Why? What's up?" Nova asked, but her smile was too wide. She knew exactly why Emory was asking.

"Eli wants me to ask you guys to come out with us tonight."

Gray came up behind his mate, his hair wet and Rieka snuggled against his bare chest. "He wanted you to ask," he said. More like he accused, as in, accused her of lying.

"Actually, he wanted me to ask everyone. But no. I'm not ready for that."

"I'm in. We going to Moe's?" Reed called over. He was leaning against his railing, eavesdropping and not showing a bit of remorse for it.

"Not you," Emory said, pointing at him without looking. "Just Gray and Nova. Please? I'd rather none of you, to be honest, but...please?"

"Why don't you want us there?" Gray asked, his brows pinching together so tight his eyes were shadowed.

"Because we just started dating and I'd kind of like to get to know him better before I bring him home to the parents, if you know what I mean. And I know you don't exactly have a lot of love for him."

"Because he's a fucking Tammen lion and he's been invading my territory for weeks, Emory," Gray said, a growl lacing his words.

"Technically, his lion was just stalking *me*," Emory pointed out, then shrugged when Gray released a soft snarl. He didn't scare or even intimidate her. But she did want his approval. She blamed daddy issues there.

"You want me to hang out with the Tammen Alpha and what? Become best bros or some shit? Drink beer after work every night?"

"Uh no. I want you to come with me tonight, show my mate some respect, and support me in my life choices," Emory said.

"Even if your life choices could get you in a shit load of trouble?"

"How? How could dating Eli could me into trouble, Gray? He's not Rhett. He's not Anson. You saw him that day. He protected us. He protected me."

"He fucking marked you, Em." Gray handed Rieka over to Nova, and Emory was reconsidering the whole not intimidated by Gray thing. Because right then, he looked a little scary. His muscles were tense, his eyes were bright blue, and she could've sworn she saw the tips of his fangs peeking out below his lips as if he was in a partial Shift. Not safe so close to Rieka.

"Maybe we should talk about this in the yard," Emory suggested, stepping back and climbing down the steps of his porch.

"Gray, calm down," Nova said, laying a hand on his forearm as he passed.

"I'm fine," Gray said, but his voice was still a little growly.

"Stalking one of my Pack members isn't any better, Em," Gray said. His voice was calm, his tone was even, but yeah...his wolf was right there in his eyes. His growl was a little softer now, but it was still there. "If I catch him here again, I will kill him."

"You know why he was doing it. You going to try to tell me if you weren't with Nova every day you and your wolf wouldn't go a little batshit crazy?"

Gray dragged a hand roughly down his face. The growl that came from his mouth that time was all human and very frustrated. "You want me to sit there and be nice," he said.

"I want you to be polite and respectful. That's all I'm asking."

Gray looked up at Nova. "Well? I know you have an opinion in all this."

Nova smiled wide. "I'll ask my dad if he can be home on time."

"We'll watch her," Callie offered. Micah looked down at her like she was nuts. "What? It'll be good practice. You're the one who's been—"

"Callie," he groaned, cutting her off before she could reveal some secret. "Fine. What time will you be home?"

Gray and Nova looked to Emory for the answer. "We'll drive separately so they can come home earlier."

"Or we could drive together so I don't have to leave you with that ass—"

"Gray," Nova stopped him.

"Fine. Separate cars."

"Yay! Let me get ready and I'll bring Rieka and her stuff over."

"Why can't they just come over here so we don't have to lug everything back and forth?" Gray grumbled.

Emory ignored the rest of their banter and ran back to her house. She checked herself in the mirror again and texted Eli. Her Alpha and his mate would be joining them, but warned him Gray wasn't thrilled about it.

I'll win him over with my charm.

Save the charm for me. She added a winking emoji and wondered if he'd read into the text as naughty as she'd meant it.

When he sent back an emoji with its tongue out, she smiled.

Emory had twenty minutes before they would head out for a double date. And she was more nervous than the first time.

Chapter Five

Eli's Mustang was already at Moe's again. This time, though, he was waiting outside when Emory followed Gray's truck into the parking lot. Eli raised his hand in a quick wave and smiled when he spotted her.

It took everything she had not to run over, wrap her arms around him, and bury her nose in his shirt. Just seeing him settled her wolf and gave her a respite from her animal's constant whining.

Emory totally got it; she was physically more comfortable just being within touching distance of her mate.

"Hey," she said, turning her cheek to give Eli access when he bent down to peck a kiss.

He straightened and offered his hand to Gray, who just sneered at it until Nova jabbed her elbow into his ribs. Gray shoved his hand into Eli's and Emory could tell he was squeezing hard by the white in his knuckles.

When he finally released Eli's hand, Eli discreetly dropped his hand to his side and clenched and flexed it a few times.

"Thanks for coming, brother. I really appreciate it," Eli said.

"I'm not your—"

"Thanks for the invite," Nova said, cutting Gray off.

Eli's hand was warm as he placed it on the small of Emory's back and led her inside. There weren't as many people packed into the tables as the night before, so they had their pick of places to sit.

As usual, they chose the table furthest from the door and jukebox so they could actually talk. Eli took the seat facing the door and Gray just stood there as if he was unsure of where to sit. Emory's Alpha always took the seat where he could watch the rest of the room.

If Eli noticed, he didn't say anything and he didn't offer up his seat. He also wasn't the one who had a slew of friends crowding the bar, watching their every move, either. Emory didn't blame him for not wanting his back to the room.

When Emory and Nova took seats across from each other, separating the men, Gray released a slow trickle of a growl and lowered into his seat, but he never really relaxed. He was just about on the edge of his seat, constantly looking around like he was expecting an ambush.

"I told my Pride to stay home tonight, if that's who you're looking for," Eli said, leaning his forearms on the table.

Gray turned to look at Eli. "I'm not worried about your fucking Pride," Gray said, his lip raising in a sneer.

"Gray," Nova whispered, her hand landing on his arm.

His eyes dropped to his mate's, but he still didn't relax.

The next thirty minutes were filled with awkward silences and forced small talk. Emory hated it. She liked the easy banter she and Eli had the night before. Even his posture was more rigid with Gray there, like he was uneasy being in the same room.

So why the hell had he told her to invite the whole Pack if he was this uncomfortable with just two of them?

"Eli, how do you like being Alpha?" Nova asked. At least this time someone was talking about something other than the heat or the upcoming Cardinals game.

"Don't really like it," Eli said.

Gray's eyes turned to Eli quickly. He looked as shocked as Emory felt.

"Why not?" Gray asked. "Those assholes not like the new laws?" Gray smirked. The jerk actually smirked like he hoped Eli would say yes.

"Not all of them, no. I've had to kick a few males out. But, no. It's just that I never wanted to be Alpha. Ever."

"So, why'd you accept it then?" Nova asked. She genuinely seemed curious.

Eli shrugged up both shoulders. "What was I supposed to do? Let someone else come in and take over? Let one of the assholes who refused to change control the Pride? Hell, there was talk of some of our family Prides coming in to step into Rhett's place. Not fucking happening." He winced and looked down at Emory. "Sorry."

She frowned up at him. "For what?" He hadn't said anything that would offend her.

"For cussing," he whispered, as if Nova and Gray couldn't hear him.

Nova and Emory both snorted then full out laughed. "It's fine, Eli. I've heard that word before," she said with a smile as she patted his arm.

So. Freaking. Cute.

"Who was your family Pride?" Gray asked, finally sitting back in his chair.

"Remsen out of southern Missouri."

The air caught in Emory's lungs. She seriously couldn't breathe. "What did you say?" she forced out around her closing throat. No way had she heard him right. No way would fate or whoever was behind this do that to her.

"My family Pride is Remsen." Eli's brows knitted together as he stared down at her. No doubt he saw the horror on her face. "Why?"

"Em?" Nova said, but there was too much blood whooshing in her ears to hear clearly. "Hey, I need to go the bathroom. Potty party?" Nova said, standing quickly and tugging Emory behind her.

Her legs felt like rubber as she stumbled behind Nova, glancing back at Eli to find him watching her.

All that fear she'd had about finding a mate. All that fear she'd had about Eli and his Pride. It all paled in comparison to the terror she felt then. All she could think was *they found me.*

****

Eli turned in his seat and watched Emory get pulled along behind the Alpha's mate. She'd looked like she was about to pass out. What the hell had happened?

"What was that all about?" Eli asked Gray.

He really hadn't expected the man to answer. Gray shrugged. "No idea," he said, narrowing his eyes at where the women disappeared. He turned his attention back to Eli, his gaze still narrowed. "They're only going to be gone for a few minutes, so I'm going to make this quick. If you hurt her, I'm going to kill you. If you're using her to fuck with my Pack, I will kill you. If you come onto my territory without an invite one more time, I. Will. Kill you."

Eli nodded. "I'm not planning to hurt her. And how the hell would I fuck with your Pack?"

"It just seems odd to me that your Alpha and his buddy Anson were all gung-ho to get Emory and you just happen to mark her. Oh, to *protect her*," Gray said, making air quotes with his fingers.

Eli leaned back in his seat and studied Gray. He respected the Alpha, but he didn't like him too much at the moment. "You think I'm full of shit," Eli said.

Eli crossed his arms over his chest and sucked his teeth. It had been his idea to invite Gray. And he was trying real fucking hard to be cool with him. But if he was accusing Eli of lying about his feelings toward Emory, they were going to have problems real fucking quick.

"You've been with Tammen for a long fucking time," Gray said. "You fought under Rhett. You followed him onto my land and attacked my Pack." He leaned forward, resting his elbow on the table. "What would you do if you were me? You've got your own Pride to look after now. You have females and cubs. Tell me how I should feel about the enemy marking one of my Pack, sneaking onto my property every night, and stalking one of my girls."

Eli opened his mouth then shut it. Fuck. He might not have a cub of his own, but he had Emory and he had Luna. Even with Emory being away from him, he knew how he'd feel if he found out some other male was creeping around checking her out. He knew how he'd feel if he found out a lion from another Pride was stalking Luna or one of his females.

A muscle jumped in his cheek and he unclenched his teeth. Gray's eyes had gone bright blue and he knew his eyes were probably pretty gold right then. The scent of fur was strong as the two Alphas stared each other down.

But Gray was right. No matter how bad it hurt him to admit it, Gray was fucking right. "I'd probably kill someone if they did that."

Gray nodded his head once. "Do her right or I won't be the only one hunting you down," he said softly, his eyes going over Eli's head.

The girls rejoined them, but Emory was still pale. "You feeling okay?" Eli asked. Maybe she was getting sick. They hadn't drank that much but maybe she was a lightweight.

"Yeah. Fine," she said curtly, avoiding eye contact.

The rest of their time together was even more forced and uncomfortable than when they'd all arrived. This night wouldn't go down in his books as a successful date, but at least he and Gray had come to some form of an agreement, even if it was a strained one.

Emory barely said more to him than yes or no and then they were all standing and saying goodnight.

"Hey," Eli said, catching up to Emory as she hurried through the tables.

He gently grabbed her arm and pulled her to a stop to a chorus of growls. Instead of glaring or telling people to back off, he released her arm and stooped so he could be eye to eye with her.

"What's going on with you? You were fine when you got here, now you can't get away from me fast enough. Did I piss you off or something?"

He wracked his brain for some offensive word or sentence he might have spewed but came up with nothing. They were mainly talking about absolutely nothing. Until Gray's mate asked about Eli's family Pride.

His eyes narrowed as he watched Emory chew on her bottom lip. Was it his family Pride that freaked her out? Why would it? They were two hours west of there. How would she know anything about them?

"It's nothing. I just don't feel well," she lied. Of course she was lying; Shifters don't get ill. They didn't catch colds. They didn't get the flu.

He turned and looked at the table they'd vacated. Okay, there were quite a few empty beer bottles, but not enough for her to be throwing up. Was it her nerves? Or was she truly, outright lying?

"Text me when you get home so I know you're safe," he said, letting it go for now.

If he knew anything about this petite woman it was she wouldn't say a damn thing if she didn't want to, no matter how much he pushed.

She nodded, but dropped her eyes and turned her back on him. He wanted to follow her out and wrap her in his arms. He wanted to feel her warmth against him. He wanted to taste her lips again. Instead, he stood just outside the door and watched as she jogged to her car, jumped in, and just about peeled out of the parking lot to get away.

Was she hurrying to get away from *him*?

Gray was watching Eli from his truck, just glaring at him, his wrists resting over the steering wheel. What had Eli missed? Maybe Gray or Nova had said something that had upset her. They were trying to keep Emory away from Eli.

His lion snarled in his head and began to pace as the Alpha started his truck, backed out, and turned onto Highway MM. He wasn't racing like Emory was. Just casually turned out of the parking lot and disappeared down the road.

Eli stood there even after the taillights were long gone and ran the night through his head. She'd been fine until he'd mentioned Remsen. He didn't remember her from his childhood, but he'd been sent to Tammen at sixteen to become an enforcer for Rhett's dad. And, she was a wolf. There was no reason she would've had anything to do with the Remsen Pride as a teenager or as an adult.

Had her family Pack gone to war with Remsen? Was that what freaked her out?

"Fuck," he ground out between his teeth.

He could question himself all night, but the only person who had the answers was Emory. And if the last twenty minutes were any indicator, he wouldn't get his answers tonight.

****

Emory's throat felt like there was something lodged as she aimed her car for home. She wouldn't cry. Not yet. She'd wait until she was inside her own house and could put a pillow over her face to muffle the sounds.

And there was no doubt there would be a lot of tears tonight.

Eli was from the Remsen Pride? That was impossible. She didn't remember him. She'd never seen him before.

Yet, she'd spent a while in that Pride.

Gray's headlights washed over the interior of her car as he caught up to her. No doubt Nova had told him everything by now. Well, everything Emory had told her which wasn't more than Jace's name and a lot of hyperventilating.

When Emory stepped out of the car, Gray was already parked and hurrying to her side.

"Emory," he barked out as she turned and jogged to her house. "We need to talk."

Fuck. She didn't want to talk. She didn't want to tell Gray anything. She just wanted to bury herself in her blankets and pillows and cry this shit out. And then, she'd figure out how to stay away from Eli for the rest of her life.

Her chest ached as her heart felt like it was splintering into a million different pieces. He didn't act like he knew why she was freaked out, but could that be exactly what he was doing? Acting? Had Remsen found her and sent Eli to bring her back?

Okay, that was stupid. He'd had plenty of chances to do that since she'd met him. Hell, he'd been creeping onto their land for weeks; at any point he could've taken off with her and her Pack wouldn't have been any wiser for hours. By then, she would've been long gone and they wouldn't have a clue where to look.

Because she'd never told them her history.

Only Tristan would have a starting point, and even he only knew so much.

"Emory!" Gray barked out as she tried to avoid the inquiry that was coming.

Emory stopped her retreat and turned to face her Alpha.

Gray was walking toward her slowly as if she were prey. His head was lowered, his eyes set on her, his hands in fists.

He was pissed.

"Gray…stop," Emory said, backing away as he advanced.

In all the time she'd been with Big River, she'd never felt the need to Shift to protect herself. But her wolf was perceiving his actions as a threat and was scratching at her skin to get out.

Shit. What the hell was he doing? What was he trying to prove?

"Gray!" Micah yelled from his porch.

Emory looked around to find her entire Pack on their porches or right in front of their houses. Great. They had an audience.

Emory glanced over at Micah as he was stepping onto the dried ground and making his way to where Gray was following Emory.

"Dude!" Reed yelled, setting down his phone and jumping over the railing. "What the fuck are you doing?"

Tristan was hurrying to stand between Gray and Emory.

"Gray, whatever you're doing right now, you need to stop. Or use your words," Nova yelled from behind him. Emory looked up at Callie, who was standing on the porch with Rieka in her arms, her eyes wide as they bounced between Emory and Gray, to where her mate was hurrying to stop Gray, to Nova, then back.

The baby began to cry, but even that didn't snap Gray out of his funk.

"I'm serious, Gray, stop." Her body was growing tighter as the trembles started. Her vision blurred and she was struggling to keep her wolf inside her body.

She didn't want to have to fight her Alpha, mainly because she knew he'd win. But another huge part was he'd beat himself up for months if he attacked the smallest member of Big River. She knew, or hoped, he wouldn't do any permanent damage to her, but pain was pain. If his teeth or claws made contact with any part of her, she'd end up injured.

She stopped dead in her tracks.

"I don't know what the fuck you're trying to do right now, but you're about to get attacked by your own Pack," Emory said, standing her ground. She tilted her head back as he got closer so she could maintain eye contact. She refused to show any form of weakness whatsoever. Not when his wolf was so riled up.

"If you fucking touch her, Gray, I'll beat your ass myself," Reed said, his voice deeper than she'd ever heard.

Tristan was directly beside her now, his shoulders an inch in front of her. Micah rounded the other side of her and flanked her left side.

Gray stopped his advance, but continued to glare at Emory. She'd never seen him like this, at least not with her. She'd seen him pissed. She'd seen him protective. But she'd never seen him go after one of his own Pack before.

"What the fuck is going on, Gray?" Micah said, standing beside Emory.

Gray's eyes flicked over to Micah. Not Gray's eyes; his wolf's eyes. Gray was lost to his wolf, almost as lost as Micah used to get.

"Who's Jace?" Gray asked, that growl still present.

All the air whooshed from her lungs.

"Who?" She'd been right. Nova had told him about Emory's mild meltdown in the bathroom.

"Don't lie to me. Tell me about Jace," he demanded. His eyes were still too bright, but his voice was returning to its normal timbre by the second.

Emory looked to each of her Pack family, but they were watching her now, too.

"I don't want to talk about him."

Gray crossed his arms over his chest and stared down at her with a deep frown.

Callie stepped off the porch but didn't come closer as she watched her family and waited for Emory's answer.

"Jace was my mate."

She'd heard people talk about the collective energy in a group shifting but had never experienced it herself…until right then.

Her family was staring at her with mixed expressions ranging from curiosity to suspicion. All except Tristan, who looked sad.

"You had a mate?" Reed's eyes roamed to her neck and she knew what he was thinking. She had a mate and now carried another man's mark.

"It's not like what you think. I promise."

"You have no idea what I'm thinking right now," Gray said. His nostrils flared with each angry breath.

Looking each of her family members in the face, she wondered how little she could get away with telling them. She hated to think about that time in her life let alone talk about it. Tristan stood at her side still, his arms crossed over his chest. No matter what, she knew he'd take her side. He always had and always would.

"Jace was a lion from the Remsen Pride."

"I figured that much," Gray said, his hands balled into fists at his side. "What I don't get is why you never bothered to tell me you were mated to a fucking lion from one of the most violent Prides in Missouri."

Emory tilted her head to the side and stared up at him. "Just say what you're thinking, Gray, because I'm too tired to guess."

"Why did you come here?" he blurted out.

"Gray," Nova said softly, her eyes going wide.

"Did Remsen send you?"

"They don't even know about Big River. Or at least they didn't when I left."

"Remsen is your family Pride?" Nova asked.

"I'm a wolf. Remember? You've seen my animal. I'm not a fucking lion."

"Yet you were mated to one. And imbedded into Remsen," Gray said, his voice even deeper with the growl.

Shit. He wasn't calming with her confession; he was growing angrier by the second.

"I wasn't imbedded. I was a fucking breeder!" Emory yelled. Her throat hurt, but not from her outburst. She was forcing her words through the emotion that was threatening to drown her.

Nova gasped, Callie whimpered, the guys growled. And Gray's eyes turned even brighter until they were glowing.

"And that's where Eli's from," Gray growled. Not Gray. Again, his wolf was taking over, watching her, his voice scratchy and deep.

"What do you mean you were a breeder?" Callie asked.

"Don't bring my baby any closer," Gray said, pointing his finger at Callie.

"Careful," Micah said, his voice now deep and growly like Gray's.

They were falling apart and it was because of Emory. Because of her secrets.

"Em? What do you mean you were a breeder?" Callie repeated, but she'd stopped moving closer. Instead, she took a few steps back, Rieka held tightly against her chest as the baby fussed.

All eyes were on Emory, Gray was trembling slightly, and Emory's wolf was pacing in her head, waiting to break through if she was needed.

Shit. She really didn't want to talk about this. She just wanted to hit the rewind button, not invite Gray and Nova on her date, and live obliviously ever after.

"I was given to Jace as a gift. I was an orphan and deadweight for my Pack. I was supposed to pop out a bunch of babies for him."

"And?" Reed asked. "What happened? Where is that fucker now?"

Emory shrugged up her shoulders. "I don't know. That was a long time ago."

"Bullshit. I need the truth right fucking now, Emory. Why did you come here of all places? What does Remsen want from us?" Gray demanded.

Anger bubbled inside of Emory until she thought she'd explode. "Do you think I'm some kind of fucking spy, Gray? You want to know what happened? I was handed over to a lion Pride at fourteen years old, beat, starved, tortured…almost raped. At fourteen. Fuck you and your accusations. I left without any help from anyone. I attacked Jace one night, and while he was down, I ran for my fucking life. And kept running until I met Tristan. And then you guys."

Tears were streaming down Emory's face. She looked around. Tears were streaming down Callie's and Nova's faces, too. Reed looked sick. Micah and Gray looked murderous. Tristan looked like he was reliving the moment he met a skinny sixteen-year-old Emory.

"Was Eli there when this was happening?" Reed asked.

Emory glanced at him and took a step back. Reed had become like a brother to her. He made her laugh harder than anyone ever had. But in that second, she feared for anyone who crossed him. His eyes were glowing as brightly as Gray's and Micah's. His body was tense, his muscles bunched as if he was on the verge of a Shift.

"I don't remember him. It was a long time ago, and I was kept separate from the other females because I always fought so much. If he was there, I never saw him."

Reed shoved his hand through his hair and scrubbed it over his scalp. "Mother fucker. Why would you keep that from me? Why would you keep that from us?"

"Because it's over. It's in my past. And I don't really like to think about it, let alone say out loud that I had no one who gave a shit about me past my uterus."

"That's why you don't want kids?" Nova asked, tears still rolling down her cheeks, glistening in the moonlight.

Emory nodded. "Yeah. I want to be worth more to someone than that."

"You are worth more," Callie said, her voice thick with emotion.

"I know what I'm worth to you guys. But…I don't just want to be a vessel for life. That probably doesn't make sense to any of you, but…yeah. I don't have any desire to get pregnant or breed for any man."

Gray had taken a step back, but his eyes were still bright. "So Eli's family Pride was no different from Tammen," he said and dragged a hand down is face. "You still don't think he's like them?"

She couldn't answer. Because, the reality was, she didn't know. Since she'd met him, he'd seemed upfront and honest with her. He'd seemed to truly care about her and the females in his Pride. But what were the chances the apple would've fallen that far from the tree? What were the chances he'd live with two separate Prides with the exact same thoughts towards women and not come out the same damn way?

"I'm so sorry," Nova said. She crossed the space between them and pulled Emory into her arms, hugging her tightly, a soft sob wracking her body.

Nova released her, took little Rieka from Callie's arms, and went into her house. The lights came on a second later and Emory could hear Nova sniffling inside.

"I need to talk to Eli," Gray said.

"I think we all do," Reed said.

"No, guys. This is my business."

"You're our business, Em. If this mother fucker was sent by your former...fuck, I can't call him your mate. If that mother fucker thinks he's going to drag you back to your former slave owner, he'll have to go through me," Gray said.

"Me first," Tristan said with a nod.

"Fuck, he'll have to go through every single one of us, Blackwater, and Ravenwood," Micah said.

Now Emory was tearing up for a whole new reason. Even if they still suspected her as some kind of tiny, child-sized spy, they had her back. They'd protect her no matter what. There was no way she could put them through more bullshit, though. Not after what they'd already gone through. Not with little Rieka there.

"I'm sorry," Gray said gruffly, his lips in a thin line.

"There's nothing to be sorry for. It's over. It's in the past." And she hoped it stayed that way.

"I'm sorry for being a dick. I'm sorry for accusing you of being a traitor," Gray said, taking a slow step toward her.

"You didn't exactly call me a traitor," she said, smiling through her tears.

When Emory didn't protest to him coming closer, he did like Nova and pulled her into a rib cracking hug.

"I'll kill anyone who tries to hurt you. You know that, right?" he whispered against her hair.

She nodded, her face rubbing the cotton of his t-shirt.

Gray kissed the top of her head, pulled away from her, and walked away, never looking back as he climbed his stairs and stepped inside to console his mate.

It was just Emory, Reed, Tristan, Micah, and Callie. The guys stood there, shuffling their feet, avoiding her eyes. But Callie looked absolutely wrecked.

"They didn't touch you, either?" Callie asked, her voice so soft and small.

"No."

"That's why you were so curious about my time with Tammen," Callie said.

Emory just nodded. That stupid emotion was bubbling back up again and her throat was getting tight.

"You kicked his ass?" Callie asked, a smile playing at the corners of her lips.

"Fucked him up," she said with a proud smile. She'd fought him in both her human and wolf form. She'd done enough damage that she'd had time to run away. She might be small, but she'd always been able to take care of herself, no matter what.

"Good," Callie said and hugged her. "Let's go," she told Micah.

Micah stood there staring at Emory for a few more seconds. "If he hurts you, Gray is the last of his concerns." He nodded once, turned, and followed Callie into their house.

Micah didn't say Eli's name, but she knew who he was talking about. In fact, she could insert any male's name in that sentence and she knew it would be the same. Micah, like Reed, Gray, and Tristan, would always have her back.

Reed left without another word. Just ruffled her hair. But she'd caught the moisture in his eyes before he turned. His heart was breaking for Emory's past just as much as the anger was riling all their animals about her possible future.

Then it was just Emory and Tristan. "Now they know," Tristan said, a closed-lip smirk on his face. "Better now?"

"Do I feel better? Not really, Tris. I thought Eli was my real mate. Not someone forced on me, but someone I could grow a life with. And no matter how hard I try to convince myself it's all a big, fat lie, my wolf is still pining for him. I still want him."

"Ask him."

"You know, there are a lot of times I wish you'd just tell everyone your truth so I don't have to work around your two-word riddles."

He snorted, shoved her shoulder, and went inside.

Emory walked over to her house and sat on the front porch. What the hell was she supposed to do now? Just tell Eli the truth about her past and find out if he knew anything about it? And what if he did? What if he'd known who she was? What if he'd known about her when she was there and did nothing to help her?

He'd been a kid, just like she'd been back then, but he could've done something. Anything. *And gone against his own family.*

Ugh. She hated this constant arguing in her own head lately. She'd never been this confused. She'd always known who she was and what she wanted from life. And now, she wanted Eli. But...she was scared and confused. If it turned out he had known about her, then what? She'd have to walk away from him and be miserable.

She'd told Tristan she'd thought he was her real mate. That was a half-truth. She *knew* he was her real mate. He was the male she was supposed to be with. He was the male her animal had chosen. He was the missing piece to her heart.

Emory had always been strong. She'd always been independent, confident, knew what she wanted and how to get it. Now, she wondered if she'd be strong enough to walk away and live the rest of her life with that big piece ripped away forever.

Chapter Six

Emory lied in bed, a pillow hugged against her chest. Eli had texted her three times last night. The last one warned he was about to come to her house to make sure she was safe. And she'd had zero doubts he'd do that.

After what she'd told her Pack, that would be the worst thing he could possibly do. So, she'd sent him a text that she was home, safe, and going to bed. And then she'd turned her phone off. That morning, there'd been four more texts waiting for her when she woke up after her measly three hours of sleep.

Is everything okay? Did I do something?

Please talk to me. If I did something, I want to fix it.

Goodnight.

Mildly clingy, but he'd gotten the hint. But she couldn't ignore him forever. She had to talk to him. She had to tell him everything and find out the truth. Otherwise, she was going to make herself nuts wondering.

Emory sent Eli a text that she'd turned her phone off the night before and promised to call him later. She had to work that day and, as tired as she was, didn't need the extra stress of a possibly depressing phone call piled on top. She just wanted to get through the day and then rip the band-aid off.

Or, maybe she'd be stitching up some rips and tears to her heart. She had to think that way. She had to stay as positive as possible and just get through her work day without snapping at anyone or letting her wolf get too close to the surface. The last thing she or any of the hundreds of Shifters in the state needed was her outing them to humans simply because she had no control over her emotions.

The day went as expected, customers asking questions, her loading bags of feed onto the shelves–and pretending they were heavy when anyone saw her–and then it was time to clock out. This was a rare circumstance when she was tempted to ask for overtime, just for an excuse to put off the inevitable.

Emory was no coward, though. She just had to get in her car, call Eli, and get it over with. No. She'd ask him to meet her. That way, he'd have to look into her eyes when he lied to her.

And there she was, once again assuming the worst.

When had things become so hazy? When had her perfectly planned life been tossed on its head? Stupid question. She knew exactly when–the night Eli followed Callie to Big River.

Sitting in her car, she turned the engine over and silenced the radio. And then she stared at her phone. Should she call him or text him? She wanted to hear his voice, but she'd made up her mind about the conversation. It needed to be done face to face. She needed to see his eyes, not just to make sure he was being honest, but because her animal was driving her batshit crazy.

"Hey," she said when she pulled her big girl panties up and hit his number.

"Hey you," he said, his voice rumbling over the line. "You okay? You had me a little worried last night."

She smiled as she watched an elderly couple push their cart to their car. All these humans around her every day and they had no idea she had an animal inside of her. Which was why she'd only ever dated other Shifters.

Now, there was more to this dating thing than just getting laid or being lonely. Eli was hers, whether she liked it or not. And she was his. And now, one word from him could ruin it all.

"Can you meet me? Like now?" She had no idea if he was at work or busy. But the longer she put this off, the harder it would be.

"Hold on," he said, and then the phone sounded staticky, like he was holding it against his chest as he spoke to someone in the background. She could hear his deep voice through his chest, but couldn't quite make out the words.

Emory watched people pull into the parking lot, park, and hurry inside her place of employment. After a few seconds, Eli came back on the line.

"Yeah. I can meet you in about ten minutes. Is that cool?"

"Yeah. Can you meet me at Hammers?"

"I thought it was closed," he said.

She smiled softly at the way just his voice calmed her.

"It is. But we can meet in the parking lot."

He was quiet for a few seconds. "So, we'll be seen," he said.

There was a tinge of hurt in his voice, but she couldn't focus on that. She had bigger fish to fry and Eli's feelings being hurt weren't even on the list.

"You there now?"

She shook her head. "No. But I just got off work so I can head over there now."

"Yeah. I'll see you in ten minutes." There was a beat of silence, then, "I thought you were gone."

Emory sighed heavily. Not yet. "See you in ten." She ended the call before she ended up telling him everything over the phone. This wasn't the kind of conversation they could have while he was on a ten-minute break. And she could tell he was either at work or hanging out with someone.

Hopefully, another male.

Eli was already there leaning against the side of his truck when she pulled into the lot. He lifted his hand and forced a smile.

Taking a deep, calming breath, Emory pushed the door open and stepped around to stand in front of him, but kept enough distance between them.

Eli watched her expectantly, something akin to fear in his pretty eyes. He crossed his arms over his broad chest and waited.

"You said you're from Remsen," she said. "When was the last time you went there?"

His brows knitted together. "About twelve years. I haven't been back there since I was sent away at sixteen." His eyes narrowed. "Why?"

Shit. Not only was she about to find out whether this whole thing was one big fucking ploy to drag her back to the people who'd almost broken her, but she was about to tell him the same things she'd told her Pack the night before. She was about to break her heart wide open again and let him have a peek inside.

"Do you know a male name Jace Washington?"

She wanted him to say no so badly. In fact, she wanted him to tell her he was mistaken and that Remsen wasn't his family Pride. She wanted to go back in time and delete that entire conversation.

His frown deepened into a scowl.

"How do you know Jace?"

Well, shit. There went those pipe dreams.

"So, you know him."

"I knew him when I was a kid. I just told you I haven't been back there or talked to anyone from that fucking Pride in twelve years." Eli pushed off his truck and took a step closer. "How do you know Jace? Or anyone from that Pride, Em?"

Tears burned the back of her eyes as she stared up into his face. She didn't want to tell him. She didn't want him to know about her past. She really didn't want to find out he'd known about her and had done nothing.

What if he had? What then? Would he even tell her the truth? She hadn't sensed any lies on him yet, but that didn't mean he wouldn't start now.

"Did you know me before that night Callie came to us?" she asked, swallowing the emotion down as it tightened her throat.

His brows popped up and his head snapped back. "No. I mean, I'd seen you around with Big River, but I don't think we ever talked before that."

"I mean, had you ever heard my name before then?"

"Emory, just tell me what the hell is going on. How do you know Jace, how do you know Remsen, and how the hell would I have known you before?"

"Jace was my mate."

A breath whooshed from his lungs and his face went slack.

"You're mated?" She continued to stare at him. "You have a mate already? Jace Washington is your fucking mate?"

His voice was going all growly.

"He *was* my mate," she corrected him.

"That's not how it works, Em. He is or he isn't." Anger turned his eyes bright gold and his nostrils flared.

"You know that's not exactly how it works with your kind."

His eyes flashed brighter and he looked like she'd hit him.

"My kind," he repeated.

She nodded. "I didn't choose Jace. He was chosen for me at fourteen years old. He was assigned my mate. That's all."

His eyes roamed her body from head to toe. "Did he leave his mark on you?"

Oooh. His voice was deep. Deeper than she'd ever heard from him.

"Against my will."

"Show me."

"I can't."

"Why not?"

She pushed the hair out of her eyes as the wind picked up, blowing dust around them. "It was forced on me while I was fighting three of them."

His eyes moved lower down her body and he nodded real slowly. "Under your clothes."

"Under my clothes," she confirmed.

"Did he…" He squeezed his eyes shut and asked the next question without looking at her. "Did he touch you?"

When she didn't answer, he peeled his lids back and stared at her, a stricken expression deep in his eyes.

Shaking her head, she said, "Not the way you think."

"He didn't rape you?" More growl in his voice.

"Eli," she warned, looking around. There weren't any people close to them, but there were cars coming and going from the small strip of stores and people were milling around in the parking lot. If he freaked out and his lion broke free, all their secrets would be blown to hell.

Eli took a few deep breaths, in through his nose, out through his mouth. When he looked back up at her, his eyes were still bright, but they weren't glowing.

"Maybe we should do this another time. Or somewhere not so…filled with humans."

"Moe's?" he suggested.

She definitely didn't want to go there. Even if every single person she knew wasn't there already, Noah would be behind the bar. And he'd be listening to every single word said between the two of them.

"No. We're fine here, just keep your animal under wraps." She smiled in an attempt to ease the situation, but he didn't smile back.

"Tell me what happened," he said, and then dragged his hand down his face. "Maybe that's not a good idea if I'm supposed to be staying calm and all that."

"I just need to know if you knew about it. Did you know what they were doing to girls?"

"I mean, I knew females were being sold and brought in by other groups, but I had no idea you were being…wait…what are you asking me? Do you think I would've let them mistreat you if I'd known you were there?"

"You wouldn't have known who I was then," she said with a small shrug.

"Do you really think I'm the kind of person who would let any female get raped if there was something I could do about it?"

"You were a kid," she said, losing a little of her fight.

"I would not let that happen, Em," he said, his voice a little loud. He caught himself and looked around to see if he'd grabbed the attention of the humans over at the store. "Even if I was a kid back then, I would never stand by and let a man hurt a woman in front of me."

Emory wrapped her arms around herself and leaned her head against the side of the car. That little bit made her feel better, but there were still so many things standing between them.

"Are they looking for you?" he asked. He'd figured out on his own that she hadn't been let go, that she'd escaped.

"I don't know. If they are, they're not looking too hard. Maybe they think I'm dead or got grabbed by another group."

"How did you survive on your own for so long? An unmated, young Shifter female would be a fucking treasure to some groups."

"I wasn't alone. I had Tristan."

He nodded and pulled his lips into his mouth as he turned everything over in his head. "That explains the way he acts around you."

"Yeah. It was just me and Tristan for a long time. Until we found Gray and Big River."

"You love him," he said rather than asked.

"Of course I do. He was my first family ever. We were there for each other when there was no one else. Are you seriously getting jealous?" Seriously? After everything she told him, her relationship with Tristan was what he wanted to focus on?

"I'm just trying to–"

"He was the first male in my life who didn't beat me or torture me or try to force himself in my pants." She pushed away from the car and stomped from the bumper to the hood and back.

"They beat you?"

"Yeah. A lot. Jace's mark isn't the only scar I carry."

His nostrils flared, his eyes glowed instantly, and he turned and planted his fist against the bed of his truck, creating a pretty impressive sized dent. He threw his head back and bellowed, the sound tapering off into a growl.

"Eli," she warned, looking up at the people who'd stopped to watch them.

"I'm not jealous," he snarled, his canines peeking below his lips. "I was trying to change subjects for a second until my lion calmed down." She'd never heard someone sound so human and so animal at the same time. It was terrifying and fascinating.

"That part of my life is over, Eli. It's in the past. I'm fine."

"You're not fine. You're covered in marks given to you by men who didn't give you the choice. Including mine."

He wrapped his arms around his middle like his stomach hurt and squatted down, resting his weight on the balls of his feet. "Fuck," he muttered. "I'm so sorry, Em."

Eli's voice was so soft it broke her heart. He was hurting for her. He was kicking his own ass because he'd caused one of those scars, because he'd done like the other men in her past and forced his mark on her.

Crouching down in front of him, she tried to force his head up with her fingers under his chin. When he jerked out of her touch, she grabbed a handful of his hair and tugged until he looked up at her, a surprised look on his face.

"Thank you," she whispered when she got his attention.

"For what? For being no better than those other fucks?"

"You actually hate what you did, even if our animals already recognized each other, even if this whole thing," she said, waving her hand between them, "was destined to happen one way or another."

"You okay, ma'am?" a male voice called out.

They both lunged to their feet, but Eli turned his back on the guy standing a few yards away to hide his glowing eyes.

"Yeah. We're fine. Just a little car trouble," Emory lied.

His eyes were narrowed as he stared at Eli's back. "Is *he* giving you trouble?" he asked, nodding toward Eli.

Emory snorted and waved her hand in the air dismissively. "No. He's just mad he didn't fix it right the first time." Wow. She'd always been a terrible liar, but it was coming easily this time.

The guys eyes bounced between Emory and Eli a few more times, then he nodded and headed back across the street to the shopping center. Even if she had a problem with Eli, there was nothing the older human man could've done about it. She'd have more luck in a fight against the big Shifter than that guy would.

"He's gone," Emory said when the guy was far enough away he wouldn't see Eli's golden eyes.

When Eli turned back around, he was trembling lightly. His lion was close, but Eli still had a little control.

"They hurt you," he said.

"Yeah."

"I won't let anyone hurt you again."

"I know."

"I'm serious, Em. I know we're new at all this and I know I'll have to earn your trust, but I promise you, if those mother fuckers ever get it in their head to come looking for you, if Jace ever tries to find you, I'll kill every last one of them."

She had no doubt he'd try. And she had no doubt her Pack and the bears and panthers would fight beside him. She just hoped Jace and rest of Remsen had forgotten all about her by now.

As long as she continued to stay off their radar, she knew there was nothing to worry about. She also knew Eli's protection didn't stop at just his former Pride. He was trying to tell her he'd keep her safe against any and all threats. And didn't that just make her feel all warm and fuzzy inside.

Eli took a tentative step toward her, so she closed the space and stepped into his bubble, wrapping her arms around his waist and breathing him in. He smelled like grease, and exhaust, and Eli.

His arms were gentle as they snaked around her back and his hands landed on her spine. One hand cupped the back of her head while the other stayed pressed against her, pulling her closer.

"Hey," she said without pulling away. "What do you do?"

"Hm?"

"Are you a mechanic?" That would definitely explain his smell and his dark hands and black fingernails he was sporting at the moment.

"Yeah. Over at Dodson's. It's owned by Tammen. Well, an older guy from Tammen. Worked there for years."

"What's your last name?"

He chuckled, the sound deep and rumbly through his chest. "Guess we don't know a whole lot about each other." His breath rasped through his chest and his body expanded against her. "Reese. Elijah Alexander Reese."

"Emory Belle Jamison. Nice to meet you."

"Your middle name is Belle?" he asked, another chuckle in his voice.

Emory pulled back, but kept her arms wrapped tightly around him. "Yeah? So?"

"Alexander Bell?" he said, his brows raised.

"Oh great. Maybe let's not tell Reed." She could just imagine the teasing she'd get from the jokester of the group.

They stood like that for long enough that the sun began to dip behind the trees. "I should get going," she said, not really wanting to pull away. It felt so good in his arms. Now that she knew he wasn't sent to bring her back to Jace, she just wanted to spend as much time as possible touching him, holding him, getting to know everything about him.

"You want to go out tonight?" he asked.

"You going to invite my Pack again?" She raised one brow at him.

"Hey, I had fun until you freaked out and ran to the bathroom."

"No you did not. No one could consider last night fun."

"I got to see you. That's all I wanted."

"Awww," she teased.

He was staring down at her, his eyes bouncing between hers, and all she wanted was to feel his lips. Now that the imminent threat of having her heart stomped into the ground was over, she wanted to try to pick back up where they left off.

Instead of waiting for him to make the move, she grabbed him by the back of his head, lifted on to her tiptoes, and dragged his head down to hers. He smiled as their lips met, leaving a soft peck before pulling back and smiling again.

"I was honestly scared I'd never get to do that again," he said against her lips before planting a slower kiss.

Pressing herself as close as she could, she slanted her head and swiped her tongue against the seam of his lips. He opened for her and she about cried out when their tongues met. There was something so perfect about the way he kissed. Or maybe it was just their connection that made everything feel perfect. Regardless, she couldn't get enough.

Just as Eli deepened the kiss, the mood was shattered all to hell.

"Get a room," a familiar voice called across the space between them and the store.

With a groan, she pulled away and shook her head at Reed, who was watching them. Even with his tease, his eyes were serious. He held several plastic bags from both arms.

"We're cooking out tonight," he called over before turning on his heel and heading to his truck where Callie and Nova waited.

Nova lifted her hand in a thumbs up while Callie just gave her a tight-lipped smile. Emory could understand her distrust of Eli and all male lions. Eli would just have to prove to her family he wasn't like the rest of them.

"I have to get back to work," he said with a heavy sigh. His hand lifted and he cupped the side of her face, his thumb gently raking over her skin. "Call me after your little family get together. I'll meet you anywhere you want. I just want to see you again tonight."

How pathetic of them was it that they were standing there, staring into each other's eyes, yet it wasn't enough. She felt the same strong need to see him again that night, too. She wanted to talk to him more. She wanted to feel his lips. She wanted to feel his hands on her body.

That thought had her pulling away from him and dipping her face to hide the blush she knew was there. Where could they even have sex? He wasn't currently welcome to Big River and she wasn't sure she was brave enough to go to Tammen territory. Not alone.

Well, she wouldn't be alone. She'd have Eli. And the other females who were learning to walk on their own two feet. Still. She wasn't quite brave enough to just wander through their streets, right up to Eli's door, for a booty call.

Not to mention, there were three other women living within his walls and he currently didn't have a bedroom. He'd said he'd given it to his sister. She had no desire to bang on the couch where anyone could find them and she'd never been much into back seat loving.

"What are you blushing about?" he asked with a crooked smile.

She could either make something up or... "Since we're mates and all, at some point, I would like to see you naked."

"You've seen me naked." Now, his smile was cocky.

Yep. She'd seen him naked. And she'd seen something she wanted enough to make her body warm. "What I mean is, we have nowhere private."

He looked at his truck, then dipped at the knees to look at the backseat of her car.

"Nope. Not happening, Eli." She slapped his arm and giggled. Actually freaking giggled. This man was sending her on an emotional rollercoaster and she loved it. She loved how he could bring out so many strong emotions in her without even trying.

Eh. She didn't love the fear she'd had when she'd thought he was some kind of plant for Remsen, but making up could be fun, too. Even if they hadn't actually fought.

Eli's smile faded and his eyes roamed her face. "I've wanted to make love to you since the day we met."

"Of course you did. You're a guy."

He snorted. "You saying you didn't think about it?"

All the dirty fantasies she'd had about Eli, even before she saw his dick, came rushing to her mind.

"Shut up," she muttered, nudging him with her shoulder.

"That's what I thought. It'll happen, Em. I'll make it happen."

"You sure are full of promises today."

He shrugged and pulled her in for another hug before they parted ways. "I'd promise the world if it made you happy."

"Corny…but feel free to say stuff like that anytime."

He squeezed and she gripped his shirt in both hands, wanting to stay right there forever. A horn honking made them part and she waved impatiently at Reed as he passed, his eyes glued to Eli.

Maybe her Pack didn't accept Eli or like that she was mated to him, but they'd come around. One way or another.

"I'll call you later," she said, lifting onto her toes for one more kiss. She needed that to hold her over until she could see him again.

He pulled away with one of those sexy smacks and winked down at her. "Call me as soon as you can."

He backed toward his truck, watching her as she rounded her car and dropped into the driver's seat. He didn't get into his own vehicle until she was pulling away, giving him a much friendlier wave.

How had her life changed so much in such a short time? When she'd realized that her animal was begging for Eli, it had freaked her out. Nah. It scared the hell out of her. Now, she couldn't wait to hear his voice again.

She'd rejected the fact he'd left his mark on her, that he'd tied them physically with the change in her blood. Now, she was thankful for it. While Jace's bite was nothing more than a show of dominance and claim, he wasn't her true mate. His mark would do nothing to her physical chemistry. She knew by the difference she felt, by the way other Shifters reacted, that she was changed from the inside out.

Eli wasn't who she would've chosen for herself. He was a lion. He was from two different violent, woman abusing Prides. But Eli the man was incredible. He was sweet and kind and protective. He cared for the people around him. He cared for the females of his Pride. He protected them and took care of them in ways no one had done for them before.

When she got home, she had to park a little further away than normal. Three of the Blackwater bears were there, their trucks lined up beside Big River's vehicles. Reed wasn't kidding about a cookout. For some reason, she'd thought it would just be her Pack.

Part of her was tempted to send a text to Nova and Reed to keep their mouths shut about what she'd told them last night. Nah. No way would her family tell her secrets like that. It was one thing for everyone to be up at arms about her dating Eli. It was completely different to divulge her darkest time.

"Hey girl," Colton said as she left her car and roamed closer to the firepit. "How'd the rest of last night go?" He chuckled and lifted his chin to Gray.

"What do you mean?" Anger rose deep inside of her. After everything, had Gray told their friends everything? And was this some kind of big joke to them?

"You looked like you couldn't get out of there fast enough last night. Already tired of the lion?" He pulled her in for a hug, but she couldn't relax into it.

"Oh. No. I wasn't feeling well last night," she said, warning Gray with her eyes.

He held up both hands and raised his brows in feigned innocence.

"Yeah. Okay. Reed said he saw you two together, sucking face in the parking lot like a couple of teenagers."

Emory pulled out of Colton's hug and took an empty chair next to Nova. "Thanks, Reed," she said with a glare.

"What? You were," he said, putting his arms out like he was holding an imaginary woman and made a kissing face complete with sounds.

"You're an idiot," Emory said, relaxing into their normal banter.

She'd much rather them give her shit about public displays of affection over lecturing her about her choice in men.

"Maybe. But I'm not the one letting a lion feel me up while people watch," Reed said, sitting back with a satisfied smile.

"Dude, were you two going around the bases in the parking lot and I missed it?" Nova said, her eyes as wide as her smile.

"You really are a perv," Emory said with a shake of her head.

The rest of the time with her friends was spent talking about anything and everything but her kissing Eli. In fact, no one even brought him or Tammen up again for the rest of the night. For the few hours, it was back to normal.

Well, as normal as her friends and family could get.

Chapter Seven

Eli had a hard time focusing on his work as images of Emory played in his brain. Fuck, she was sexy. Did she even realize she moaned when they kissed? He was just as hard now as he was then. Of course, that probably had to do with her mention of wanting to have sex with him.

Adjusting himself and pushing his boner to the side to keep from getting squeezed by his zipper, he grabbed a wrench and messed with the engine he'd been working on.

"Dude. You still on that same piece of shit?" the shop's owner, Chuck, asked. He stood behind Eli, his arms crossed over his chest, his gray brows pulled low.

Even being older and set in his ways, Chuck had been supportive of the new laws. He had a daughter. He'd never approve of anyone treating her the way the lionesses of Tammen were treated.

"Got distracted," Eli admitted, ducking back under the hood.

"By that pretty little wolf?" Chuck asked.

Eli stood up straight. How the hell did Chuck know about Emory?

"Don't look surprised. You two aren't exactly being sneaky," Chuck said, grabbing a rag from on top of Eli's tool box and wiping away a thick layer of grease from the palms of his hands.

"Everyone knows about her?" Eli asked, leaning one hand against the side of the car.

"Anyone who's been paying attention. You paraded her around at Moe's."

"I wasn't parading her around. We were on a date," Eli said. He wasn't the kind of guy who needed everyone to know Emory was his.

"Where you knew there would be Pride members hanging out," Chuck said.

"Actually, she chose it. I think she felt better being around people who'd watch out for her."

"She doesn't trust you," Chuck said.

"Would you? Our Pride is fucked up. Look at what they did to that council guy."

Chuck shook his head. "Nope. Not our Pride. Just a few guys. Most of them are gone now. She needs to know that."

"I've told her."

Eli leaned back over and continued to try to loosen the same nut he'd just tightened. Fuck. His brain was too locked on Emory to focus on anything else.

"How the hell do I convince her, Chuck?"

The lions didn't have elders. They had an Alpha and that was it. So the fact the current Alpha was asking advice from another lion was huge. And Chuck knew that.

A tiny smile ghosted his lips and he all but puffed up with pride that he'd be asked for his thoughts. "You'll just have to show her. Get her over. Introduce her to the lionesses."

Eli snorted. "You think that's a good idea? Just because some of the assholes are gone doesn't mean all of them are."

"So, fix that. Get them on the same page or send them packing."

"I don't want to be that kind of Alpha. I don't want to be a dictator."

Chuck stepped closer and put a hand on Eli's shoulder. "A good leader isn't the same thing as a dictator. Your job is to protect those ladies. The guys can take care of themselves, but you have to teach them the right way. You're doing a good job, Elijah."

Eli nodded over and over as he listened to the older guy. He'd always liked Chuck. Had always respected him. His encouragement meant more than Eli realized it would.

"Thanks, Chuck," he said, dipping his head once. "That means a lot."

"Go home. You ain't gonna fix that hunk of junk tonight. Not with that little girl on your brain."

Eli huffed out a laugh. Eli might be in charge at home, but this was Chuck's garage. He could do and say what he wanted, including sending his Alpha home for being out of his mind in love.

Stopping with his hand halfway into the tool box, he stared at Chuck's retreating back. In love? Was he actually falling in love with his mate? He was obsessed with her, cared a lot about her, felt like he'd burn the world down to protect her, but did he love her?

Her laugh echoed through his mind. Yeah. He did. He might not say that to her. It'd freak her out and she didn't need any more shit scaring her. But yeah…he was falling hard for the tiny woman. He knew he'd do anything and everything to make her happy, no matter what it would cost him.

He'd even walk away from Tammen if that was truly what she wanted.

****

Emory stood on her porch, waving at the guys as they left Big River. Her phone was heavy in her back pocket as she waited for some privacy to call Eli. It was too late to meet up now. She'd wanted to excuse herself and go see him, but she knew she'd never hear the end of it from her Pack. Hell, she'd never hear the end of it from Colton.

The second everyone headed to their own houses, she hurried through her door and pulled her phone out, hitting Eli's number that she'd changed from his name to Mate.

He answered on the first ring.

"Hey. Sorry I didn't call earlier. All of Blackwater was here."

"Don't worry about it…I missed you," he said.

She gripped the phone between her shoulder and cheek and laid onto her back, throwing her arm over her head. Déjà vu. It felt like they'd had this very same conversation not that long ago.

"I kind of missed you, too," she whispered and smiled into the dark. She hadn't bothered to turn on any lights, still hadn't taken off her clothes for the day. She liked that she could still smell Eli on her. She loved that his scent was embedded in every fiber of her clothing and every fiber of her being.

His heavy sigh caused static over the line and all Emory could do was smile. She loved that sound. It was so stupid, but she knew it was a contented sigh, much like she'd done before she'd found out about Remsen.

Now that she knew he wasn't in cahoots, so to speak, with any of them, she wanted to get back to that feeling, that girly, brand-spanking-new-relationship giddiness she'd had after their first date.

"You should've seen me at work after you left," Eli said.

Emory could almost picture his smile as he spoke.

"What happened? You get in trouble for being late getting back?"

He snorted. "I might not own the place, but I'm still Alpha. I don't get in trouble."

"Oooh, aren't we cocky," she teased.

"No; I didn't get in trouble. I couldn't remember what I was doing while I was doing it. I couldn't stop thinking about you…about that kiss."

"Not the first time we've kissed, Eli."

Her smile was wide as she rolled over onto her stomach and kicked her heels up behind her like a freaking high school girl on the phone with her first boyfriend.

"It wasn't just the kiss," he said.

He was definitely thinking about the fact she'd brought up sex. If he'd been like her, he'd been horny since they separated. If it was possible for women to have blue balls, she was sporting quite a pair at the moment.

"Yeah?" she asked, trying her best to sound sexy and coy. Not exactly her strongest traits.

"You've got me thinking about you naked."

Emory closed her eyes and savored those words. Technically, he'd already seen her naked. But, with what was going on at the time, he might not have bothered checking her out. Wasn't like when he'd come wandering out of the woods with his big dick swinging in the air.

"Are you trying to have phone sex with me?" she asked.

She rolled onto her back and immediately undid the button in her jeans. She could pretend all she wanted, she could play hard to get until she was blue in the face, but the second he started talking dirty, her hand was going down her pants. No way would she spend the next who-knew-how-long sexually frustrated.

"Gotta tell you, if that's all I can get for tonight, I'll take it." His deep chuckle met her ears and every inch of her body tightened at the sound.

Was this how Callie and Nova felt all the time? It would explain why she had to listen to Callie and Micah making love every day. From the second she'd fully accepted Eli was her mate, her body had hummed with energy. It constantly craved him. Her wolf whined and clawed at her mind, wanting more of her mate, wanting to be near him.

And all she had for the time was a phone call.

Unless...

"We could..." She inhaled and blew it out slowly through pursed lips. Was she really going to suggest this?

"We could what?" he asked, his voice husky.

"We could always meet in the woods. Just outside the Big River line. That way, you're not technically going against what Gray said. And I won't be near your Pride."

"I wish you'd trust me," he said, his tone suddenly sad.

No no no. She needed him happy and horny. Sad meant she'd go to bed wanting.

"I trust you. I don't trust the rest of the Pride," she admitted.

They were his people. He was in charge of their happiness and safety. But that didn't mean there weren't some holdovers of the old way. And the second some male treated her like a piece of meat or talked down to a female in front of her, she knew she'd lose her shit and cause problems for Eli.

Another sigh, but this wasn't the contented sigh she liked. Nope. This one was frustrated.

"Back to the midnight booty call," she teased, hoping to get his mind back to business.

Another soft chuckle. "Who owns the land?"

"No one. The bank. It's currently for sale."

Emory could hear fabric rustle over the phone. Was he lying on the couch naked? No. There were too many people living in his house for him to sleep naked. She pictured him shirtless, wearing a pair of sexy ass boxer briefs that clung to every muscle and showcased his no doubt giant boner.

"What are you doing?" she asked. Why was she so breathless?

"Putting my clothes back on," he answered. That deep, husky voice was back.

"Were you naked?"

Damn, she loved his deep chuckle.

"Aren't you a little perv?" he said.

She couldn't wait to tell Nova, the true perv, all about this conversation, and hopefully, about their first hookup. Nope. She wasn't ashamed to kiss and tell, especially when she had a feeling the first time with Eli would be epic.

"No. I wasn't completely naked. I was wearing boxers."

"Were they briefs?" she asked as her hand slowly made its way under her panties.

"Are you touching yourself?" he asked suddenly. She could imagine him sitting straight up, his eyes wide, his breath coming quickly.

"Maybe."

"Tell me where to meet you. I'll be there in five minutes."

That definitely sounded better than finishing herself off. She rattled off a location. They'd be able to pinpoint each other by scent, so she wasn't worried about not finding him once they were out there. All she was worried about was getting caught sneaking out.

"See you in five."

The call ended and her heart thundered behind her ribs. Why did all of this make her feel like a kid? She was about to sneak out, meet up with a boy, and hopefully, make it to home base. Then, she had to get back without anyone knowing she was gone.

Shit. Someone would be patrolling tonight, thanks to Eli trespassing. She had to get by whoever that was or the whole plan would be blown to bits.

Shoving her feet into a pair of tennis shoes, Emory slipped her phone into her back pocket and tiptoed out of the house.

She stood on her porch a few seconds, straining her ears for any movement. She hadn't been on the phone long, so there was a good chance someone could still be awake. All they'd have to do was look out the window and they'd see her running toward the woods. The question, though, was would they tattle?

Just the thought of getting caught trying to meet up with her boyfriend for a tryst in the middle of the night made this all the more exciting. It wasn't like anyone could do anything to her or punish her in any way. Still, she really didn't want to get any shit from Gray or Tristan. Or some major ball busting from Reed.

No sounds, but she had no idea if whoever was on tonight had already taken off to watch the perimeter or if they'd wait until later tonight. It was still fairly early, so she might have some time before anyone came outside again.

With one more check, she sprinted for the tree line and headed toward the area she'd told Eli to meet her, her heart thundering the entire way. Her smile was wide and she was almost giggling as she got farther away from the houses. As fast as she was running, she'd be to Eli within seconds.

She could hear his feet crunching over dry leaves and twigs as she ducked and dodged low hanging branches. And then she saw him, then moon casting a silver haze all around him like a freaking beacon.

Neither of them slowed, just crashed into each other, their arms going around the other one. Eli lifted her and she wrapped her legs around his waist, her lips slamming down on his, causing their teeth to bump.

It was so sexy, all of it, from the guttural sounds he was emitting to the way he couldn't stop touching her. His hands were everywhere, her ass, her back, the side of her face, cupping her breast. And then he lowered onto his knees, her body still clinging to his.

"Eli," she hummed against his lips.

He pulled away from her and trailed kisses and nips along her jaw, that little spot behind her ear, to her throat, and finally her collar bone. Her fingers were tangled in his hair as he moved lower. He released his hold on her body only long enough to peel her shirt over her head and expose her breasts.

The humid air mixed with the desire coursing through her caused goose flesh to raise across her body, until he smoothed each spot with his warm palm.

His breath was coming in pants as he frantically yanked his shirt off then unsnapped the button on his jeans. She didn't bother waiting for him to undress her; they could explore each other leisurely another time. This was all about them connecting for the first time. This was sating a soul deep hunger.

As Eli struggled with his jeans, she laid back and shimmied out of her pants, pushing them down her legs and jerking them off her feet. The second they were both naked, she grabbed him by the back of the neck and pulled him to her.

He settled between her open thighs, his weight held up on his elbows as twigs and other things jabbed her in the back. She didn't care. She didn't care if she was lying on a bed of freaking nails. Nothing could stop her making love to Eli tonight.

The second the blunt head of his cock pressed against her opening, she moaned. He hadn't even pushed into her yet and she was about to come undone. His eyes were on hers, bright gold as surely as hers were bright blue, as he pushed inch by delicious inch into her.

They moaned in unison as their hipbones finally touched.

This. Was. Everything.

Neither of them said a word; they didn't have to. Everything she needed to know was right there in his eyes, and, honestly, it scared her a little. It was so much more than lust. So much more than desire. It was affection. It was warmth.

It was love.

Emory squeezed her lids shut as tears burned the back of her eyes. How many times had she had sex with someone and never truly made love? Not until that very moment, not until Eli buried himself deep inside of her.

His hand smoothed over her hair and she looked back up at him. She wasn't positive, but she could've sworn she saw moisture glistening in the moonlight. Where their initial connection had been hurried, his hips were now moving slowly, like he was savoring every second of it.

"You okay?" he whispered.

"Perfect," she whispered back and smiled.

She meant it. She knew in her heart this moment was the most perfect moment of her life. It was something she never knew she could have but wanted more than anything. She was fully, one hundred percent connected to her mate, the man her animal and now her heart had claimed.

****

Eli had never struggled to hold back while with a woman so badly in his life. He wanted to pound into her warmth, yet he wanted this night to last forever. He'd always thought she was gorgeous. He'd found her sexy from the moment he laid eyes on her.

But lying beneath him, bared to him with the moonlight washing her in silver, her breasts heaving as she moaned with each thrust of his hips, he found her the most beautiful creature he'd ever seen.

The second she'd asked him whether he was naked, he knew he had to have her. It was just a confirmation that she was thinking about him as much as he was thinking about her. She'd also mentioned earlier that day that she'd had sex on her mind. Why else would she have brought up the living situation and the lack of privacy when making love?

And that was what they were doing. He was making love for the first time in his life. He'd finally found the one woman made for him solely. He'd worried about how it would work with her being so much smaller than he was, not to mention he wasn't exactly small in the dick department, but even though she squeezed him as he slid in, they fit like a fucking glove and hand. Everything about the two of them was like some intricate puzzle, every inch of them fitting together, even the way her breasts pressed into his pecs, the way her thighs wrapped around his hips, everything.

Fuck, he loved her. He wasn't falling in love with her; he was already head over heels, stupid in love with her. His mouth opened to say the words but he just couldn't get them out. He didn't want to scare her off. She'd had enough bullshit from men. He had to let her set her own pace, let him know when she was ready for the next step in their relationship.

She was moaning non-stop and her eyes had rolled close. And that was the last of his restraint. His hips moved faster as he pumped into her until she clenched around him, threw her head back, and whispered his name into the night air with much reverence.

Every inch of Eli's body tightened, and he buried his face in her neck and grunted. He barely had the foresight to pull from her and trap himself between their bodies before spilling onto her stomach. They'd have to be more careful next time. She didn't want kids and he wouldn't do that to her.

His chest rose and fell against hers as they gasped for air, their hearts racing to the same tempo. Their bodies were slick with sweat, the humidity in the air adding to the moisture.

Emory's arms snaked around his shoulders and hugged him tight, her lips pressed gently against the side of his neck and Eli had this insane urge to ask her to bite him. He wanted her to mark him the way her Pack did, to claim him so anyone who saw his scar would know he was hers.

"Emory?" he said, pulling back just enough so he could see into her eyes.

"Yeah."

"Will you mark me?" he asked.

Fuck it. He'd just put it out there. All she could do was say no. For some reason, though, the thought of her rejecting something that meant nothing to lions cut him a little deep. It felt as if she were to leave her claiming mark on him, she was fully accepting their bond, she was accepting him one hundred percent as her mate. And damn anyone who protested against them.

"Lions don't get marked by their females," she said, her eyes bouncing between his.

There was no emotion behind her words. She was just stating a fact. But when her eyes dropped to the point where his shoulder and neck met, he knew she'd wanted to latch onto him the whole time. That was why she'd been feathering kisses there; that was as close as she was allowing herself to get.

"We don't. But you're a wolf. Your people mark their mates. I want you to mark me as yours."

"Are you sure? Won't that freak your Pride out?"

"Do you really give a shit what anyone else thinks about us? Because I don't."

He pushed a strand of hair stuck to her face with sweat away and just stared down at her. He would never get tired of looking at her. He'd never get tired of exploring her mouth, her body, her mind.

"I don't want to cause any more trouble," she said. "We're just getting everyone to at least accept the fact we're together."

"We are together then?" he asked. Just a couple of days ago, she'd said she wanted to date and see where this would go. His heart began to race again as a slow smile spread across her face.

"Oh, we're still going to continue this dating thing. You're my mate, but I'll never jump into anything blind again."

Jace. Her mind was drifting to Jace.

Pulling away from her, and earning a groan of frustration from Emory, he sat back on his haunches and let his eyes trail the length of her body, searching for the scars left by her former mate.

There. Right on the outside of her right thigh. She must've been fighting him when he'd bitten her. It wasn't even in the right place for lions. But the fucker had been desperate and grabbed the first place he could.

Keeping the anger out of his movements, he trailed his fingertips over the silver crescents, hating the marks and the person who'd put them there more than anything in his life.

"I want to kill him," he blurted out, his eyes still on the mark.

Her hand landed on his fingers and held them there while covering the scar. "It's over. It's in the past."

"As long as that fucker is alive, I don't know if I can ever let it go. He hurt you. He forced his mark on you. He tried to…" Eli inhaled deeply and held it while he struggled to keep his lion away. Both sides of Eli wanted to leave their own mark over Jace's, then track the asshole down and make him pay.

"You'll have to let it go. If you go looking for him, they'll know where I am. And I can't bring anymore shit to Big River's steps. We've all dealt with enough to last us a lifetime."

"It would be on my Pride, not your Pack."

"I'm part of Big River, Eli. Where do you think they'll look for me?"

Eli dropped his head. She was right. He might not like it, but she was right. As long as Emory stayed off Remsen's radar, they'd probably just assume she was dead. If those assholes ever got it in their mind to seek her out, though, Eli and all of Tammen would be ready. It would be the first time he knew Big River, Blackwater, and Ravenwood would fight side by side with the lions.

Leaning forward, he pressed a soft kiss to her thigh, then laid beside her, pulling her so she was lying on his chest. He hugged her close and breathed in her scent. It was a combination of her animal, something sweet and kind of fruity mixed with the forest ground. It was heady and intoxicating.

"We should go," Emory said, but didn't bother to pull away or make any effort to get up and get dressed.

"We haven't been out here that long." As much as he hated to admit it, he hadn't lasted nearly as long as he wanted. It had been their first time and he'd gotten lost in her tight heat.

She snorted. "I wouldn't brag about that."

She was teasing him. He knew she'd come. Even if she hadn't moaned his name, he'd felt her tightened around his dick.

And with that thought, he started to get hard again. As if her words had been a challenge, he rolled them so he was cradled between her thighs again, smiling when she giggled, and sunk into her.

That time, they both lasted longer. They took their times touching and teasing, kissing and licking. Emory pushed him away, onto his back, then straddled him. He lifted his hands and cupped her tits, fighting his body's need for release. This had been one of his biggest fantasies every time he'd taken himself in his own hand. And fuck if the reality wasn't better than anything his imagination could've come up with.

Her eyes dropped to his shoulder again then up to his eyes.

"Do it, Em. Mark me as yours."

As her body began to tighten around him, she draped her upper body over him. Her lips were soft against his pulse point before she moved to the right, opened her mouth, and sank her fangs into his shoulder.

The pinch of pain sent him spiraling over the edge. She lifted quickly, then sat on his cock so he spilled onto his own stomach that time.

As she lapped at the blood seeping from her bite, his foggy brain went to one odd thought: they needed condoms. If he didn't come while cradled in her sex, he was going to lose his fucking mind.

Chapter Eight

Emory smiled the whole way back to her house. She'd finally had sex with Eli. Nope. They'd made love. Three times. The second, she'd marked him. He'd actually asked her to leave her claiming mark on him.

For a second, she'd actually feared he was going to bite her again right where Jace had. She hated that mark, but it was a daily reminder of how strong she was and how she was a survivor. She didn't want it gone, no matter how badly it pissed her mate off.

Clapping her hand over her mouth, she stifled a squeal. She was mated. For real mated. They carried each other's marks now. And all those naughty thoughts she'd had about Eli for the past few months were nothing compared to reality. Not only was he as big as she remembered, but the man knew how to please.

Shame they couldn't have enjoyed themselves in a nice comfy bed instead of getting stabbed by sticks and pinecones and whatever else littered the ground. She'd be picking leaves out of her hair for days after their little tryst.

Crunching Earth made her close her eyes and sigh as a familiar scent hit her smack in the face.

"What the hell are you doing, Em?" Reed asked as he emerged from behind a tree. "I thought I was about to get in a fight with a lion. But, no, it's just you I smelled."

He crossed his arms over his chest and leaned against the tree he'd been hiding behind. The lion he smelled. She was covered in Eli's scent from head to toe and would carry it forever now. Any Shifter within sniffing distance would not only be able to detect the change in her blood, but they'd be able to smell her mate all over her since they'd officially done the dirty deed.

"I'm currently heading home for bed. What are you doing?" she asked, attempting to loop around him so she could avoid the conversation.

"Em, stop," Reed said, way too much authority in his tone for her taste. He was following her and grabbed her by her bicep, pulling her to a stop. "What the hell are you doing? Gray told Eli to stay away so you invite him onto our land for a midnight booty call?"

Emory snorted. That had been exactly what she'd called it when she'd been telling Eli she knew a place where they could be alone for a while.

"He wasn't on our land. I made sure of that." She mimicked Reed's body language and crossed her arms over her chest. Of course, the fact she had to tilt her head back to look into his eyes took some of the intimidation away.

Reed frowned at her and then his brows shot up to his hairline as his eyes went wide. "Dude. Did you guys seriously just hook up on a piece of abandoned land? Okay…that's kind of corny movie romantic."

"Romantic?" she teased. She much rather preferred Reed being the jackass she knew and loved over the protective Pack brother.

"You know what I mean." He dropped his arms, ran a hand over his hair, then sighed. "Look, I'm trying to be open minded about all this mate shit with the lion, but…" He shrugged. "He's a fucking Tammen lion," he whispered as if anyone were around to hear them talking.

"So?"

"He's a Tammen Alpha lion," he said, widening his eyes for affect.

"Yep. Alpha. Which means he's in charge, Reed. I trust him. I just ask that you give him a shot."

"He marked you, Em. He marked you while you tried to get away. I saw it and couldn't get to you."

The pain on Reed's face at the memory about gutted Emory. He was beating himself up for not protecting her. They'd been the closest of the Pack since they'd met. He was pretty much her best friend, even if he was a guy and goofy as hell at times.

"I know," she said, her hand immediately going to the back of her neck. She laid her palm over the scar and swore it tingled at the mere mention. "You know why, though. No matter how pissed everyone is about it, he did it to protect me."

"That was part of it, but you know his lion wanted you. He forced that fucking bond."

"And it all worked out fine. Reed, look." She took a step closer. "I know you guys love me. And I know you're all worried that he'll end up like Rhett or some shit. But he's not like that. We're not like that. We're fine. He's my mate. Whether you, or I, or anyone else likes it, our animals have chosen. And to be straight with you…and I swear if you repeat this, I'll tell everyone your favorite movie is The Greatest Showman."

"It is not," he protested, lifting his head and frowning down at her.

"Oh, please. I've heard you singing the songs. Don't you think the entire Pack has heard you play that fucking movie at least a dozen times."

"That redhead is hot," he said.

"Whatever. All I'm saying is, it's beyond just our animal side at this point. I'm seriously falling in love with him."

"In three dates?" he asked, giving her an incredulous look.

"I've known him for longer than three dates."

"Oh, bullshit. Y'all barely talked to each other until you caught him playing peeping Tom."

"He wasn't looking in my windows, you dork. He was just…I don't know, protecting me from afar."

"You totally just sounded like one of those characters in Nova's books."

A sly smile pulled Emory's lips up. "You read her books? Ooooh, I'm so telling everyone if you blab a single word about tonight."

"You play dirty," he said, jabbing a finger at her. "Go home and take a shower. You look like you've been rolling around in the…damn. You two didn't even bring a blanket before you shagged in the woods." He shook his head like he was disappointed in Emory.

Shaking her head, Emory walked past Reed. "Goodnight, Reed."

He'd be on perimeter watch for the next few hours, which meant he must be off tomorrow. Unless the guys were planning on switching off at some point in the night.

No. It was Friday night. That meant the guys were off for the weekend. Did Eli get weekends off, too? Her schedule wasn't the typical Monday through Friday, but just like most of Eli's life, she had no idea whether he had a set schedule.

She was silent as a freaking mouse as she cleared the tree line and watched the houses as she moved like a ninja toward her own. Reed catching her, she could handle. What she didn't want to deal with was Tristan and his questions and accusations.

Free and clear, she made it through her front door and kicked off her shoes. She grabbed an oversized t-shirt and some shorts for bed and collapsed onto her futon, exhausted and almost boneless.

That had been the sexiest time in her life. And she couldn't wait for more with her mate.

****

It had been three days since Eli and Emory had met up in the woods and she hadn't seen him since. They'd texted and talked on the phone, sometimes late into the night, but neither of them could seem to find the time to get away to hang out.

Eli said there were things going on in his Pride, but his voice sounded off. He sounded tense, even when he was being sweet and apologizing for not being able to see her. And he hadn't invited her onto his territory. Of course, she'd been pretty clear about her opinion of his people, but she'd have thought he would've at least brought it up again.

She had this sick feeling in her stomach there were problems in his Pride and it had to do with the scar on his shoulder. Even when he was wearing a shirt, she'd bitten him to where part it would show.

By the fifth day of Eli making excuses as to why they couldn't go out, she began to wonder if she'd been used. They still talked on the phone and texted throughout the day, but why couldn't he find ten minutes out of his day to see her?

He'd gotten what he wanted from her. That was all she could think. He'd scored with the tiny wolf everyone had been after. He now had bragging rights.

Well, who the fuck did he think he was?

Glancing outside, she figured she had at least two more hours of sunlight. For some reason, going to the Pride territory didn't seem as scary with the sun out as it did at night. But even with the bright summer evening sun shining, she still wasn't sure if she could go alone. She needed backup. She needed someone with her in case shit went down.

But who?

Tristan tended to be intimidating because he never talked. No one knew what was going through his head or what he was capable of. He also held a bone deep hatred for the lions. He wouldn't be the greatest candidate for a neutral companion who could just watch her back while she tore into Eli.

She could always ask Nova or Callie, but she didn't want to pull Nova away from Rieka and wouldn't dare ask Callie to go back to Tammen. Not when she'd only been away from them for a few months.

There was always Micah or Gray, but Micah was unpredictable, especially without Callie there to keep him level. And Gray...well, Gray was still pissed about Eli's trespassing.

That left her with Reed.

While she knew she could always ask one of the bears from Blackwater, she really didn't want to pull them into something that wasn't their problem. Of course, it wasn't Reed's problem, either, but she was his friend, his sister, and this was something she needed so she could grieve the loss of who she knew was her mate.

What would she do if she got there and find out he'd lied, that he really did have a few mates? Or worse, what if the women living in his home weren't women who were trying for their independence and his sister, but they were his personal harem?

Mind made up, she slipped her feet into her boots and jogged over to Reed's. She knocked a little too hard, then smiled when she heard the ending song of Greatest Showman go silent. Busted.

"What?" he asked when he answered the door, his eyes going over her head to search for a threat.

She looked behind her and then frowned at him.

"You were pounding on my door like we were under attack by aliens or some shit."

"Really? Aliens? That was your first thought? Do you have some weird fear of little green men or something?"

He rolled his eyes. "Since we're obviously not being invaded, what do you want?"

"I need you to go to Tammen with me."

All ambient noise stopped. Every single member of her Pack heard her and stopped whatever they were doing to eavesdrop.

"I'm going to cuss out Eli, since I know everybody's listening," Emory called out, raising her voice unnecessarily.

"Oh, I'm so in for a road trip."

Reed stepped back inside and grabbed a shirt and shoes. Gray, Nova, Micah, Callie, and Tristan all stepped onto their front porches wearing matching looks of confusion and concern.

"I don't think that's a good idea," Gray said, stepping off his porch. "What happens if you're attacked?"

"That's why I'm bringing Reed," Emory said, meeting him in front of Reed's. She shoved her hands in her back pockets and tilted her head back to look into her Alpha's face. "I refuse to be made a fool by anyone, even if the asshole happens to be my mate."

"You're sure he's your mate, though, Em?" Callie asked, leaning against the railing of her porch.

Emory nodded and blinked rapidly as tears burned the back of her eyes. Stupid emotion. Stupid heart break. Stupid Eli for making her feel this way. He wouldn't get away with it. Maybe her going off on him wouldn't fix anything but it would make her feel better to let him know how pissed she was.

"He's my mate. And now, I'm going to be his worst fucking nightmare," Emory said, crossing her arms over her chest and lifting her chin.

Nova smiled and lifted a fist in the air. "Kick him in the balls," she said.

"What is with you girls always wanting to kick people in the balls?" Reed asked as he finished tying his boots.

"Reed won't be enough if the entire Pride turns on you," Gray said.

"Thanks, asshole. You calling me weak?" Reed said.

"No. I'm saying two wolves won't survive against an entire Pride." Gray looked over his shoulder at Nova. After a few seconds, Nova smiled wider and nodded. "Micah and I will come. Callie, you stay with Nova."

"Why do I always have to stay behind? I want to kick Eli's ass, too, for hurting my girl."

"Because you just got out of that place," Micah said, kissing Callie on the temple before stepping off their porch.

"I don't want you going back there either, Callie. But thanks for the ass kicking offer," Emory said with a wink.

Okay, so it looked like she'd have a full escort to put Eli on blast for being a pig.

The four of them piled into Reed's truck and then her stomach started flipping and flopping with nerves. She wasn't really scared, per se, but she seriously didn't want physical confirmation that Eli had been exactly what everyone had warned her about.

The distance between Big River and Tammen wasn't far enough to give Emory the time to calm her nerves. It didn't matter. He was going to hear her regardless of whether her voice shook or the tears she was trying to hold back escaped.

There was no one standing sentry at the gates as Reed drove right through and navigated the two streets in search of Eli's house. Shit. She had no idea where he lived.

"Hey," Reed called through the window to a guy working on his car in his driveway. The guy looked up with a frown. "Which house belongs to the Alpha?"

The guy straightened and wiped his hands on a dirty towel, his scowl permanently in place as he said, "Who the fuck are you? Why the fuck are you here?"

Micah began to growl in the seat beside her, so she reached over and swatted his leg. It wasn't the same sweet caress he got from his mate when he acted up, but she wasn't sweet like Callie, and she wasn't his mate.

"Knock it off," Emory whispered.

"I got his mate in the backseat," Reed answered, leaning on the open window as if he didn't have a care in the world. Emory knew deep down, every guy in the truck was probably hoping this dude or anyone else in the Pride would start something so they could work their frustrations out on someone's face.

The guy lifted his chin and gestured to a house centered in a semi-circle of ranch homes. They all looked the same, had the same color shutters, had identical landscaping. There'd be no way to tell each apart from each other except the numbers on the houses.

"Thanks," Reed said as he pulled away and then muttered, "Asshole," under his breath. "Charming group of people, Em."

"Shut up," she said, her eyes glued to the front door of Eli's house. That was where the similarities in the houses ended, she noticed. Their shutters were all the same color, but the doors were each a different shade or hue.

The second Reed put the truck in park, Emory took a calming breath, pushed from the back seat, and stomped right up to Eli's door. She pounded over and over until her fist began to throb.

The door swung open and Emory took a step back. Instead of Eli, a woman who stood a few inches taller than Emory with golden blonde hair and a stark scar across her cheek stood wide-eyed.

"What the hell?" the woman asked. "Who are you?"

"Is Eli home?" Emory asked, propping her fists on her hips.

The woman looked Emory over, from head to toe, then nodded. "You've got to be Emory. I thought he was exaggerating about how tiny you were. Come on in."

Emory looked behind her at the truck of her Pack brothers. If she went inside, it would take them a minute to get to her if anything happened. But she could handle herself with one lone lioness.

Emory held up her index finger, asking for a minute, and followed the woman in.

"Emory!" Reed warned.

She waved him off and closed the front door behind her, cutting off any more warnings or protests.

"I'm Luna, Eli's sister. Have a seat. He's in the shower."

At least he hadn't lied to her about Luna. So at least one woman living in his home was a relative instead of a baby maker. But that didn't make her feel much better.

"I'll stand," Emory said, leaning against the front door. She wanted to be closer to an escape route, just in case.

Luna shrugged and climbed the stairs. Seconds later, Emory heard her knock on a door.

"What?" Eli's deep voice was muffled.

"You have company."

"Tell that fucker I'll deal with him later," Eli replied.

Emory frowned up the stairs. *Was* he having issues with his Pride?

"You don't want me to do that. She's waiting downstairs."

There was silence and then the squeak of faucets preceded his thundering steps overhead. Eli came rushing down the stairs with nothing but a towel wrapped around his waist, beads of water running down his body, his wet hair sticking up in every direction.

"Emory?" he asked, a confused frown bringing his black brows low.

Her eyes ran from his head to his bare feet. He was covered in bruises, cuts, and gashes. Those were claw and tooth marks marring his skin between the fading bruising.

"What the hell happened to you? Who did this?"

A flash of anger toward her Pack and the bears made her see red.

"What are you doing here?" He took two steps toward her, but she held up her hand.

"Are you avoiding me?"

"What?"

"It's been five days since we…is that all you wanted from me? Did you use me?"

"Seriously? You still think I'm capable of something like that?"

He crossed his arms over his chest and his muscles bulged and tensed. His tattoos were darker with the water rolling down them and her mouth was suddenly dry.

Stop ogling him, Em, and tell him off.

Yet, she couldn't find the freaking words. She just kept staring at his body, horrified by the destroyed and battered flesh between each of his beautiful body art.

"What the hell happened to you, Eli?" she asked, finally raising her eyes to his.

"He's been fighting the Pride," Luna answered.

"Luna," Eli said, that deep, Alpha voice full of warning.

"Oh, whatever. You said she's your mate. That makes this her Pride, too. She deserves to know what's going on. Or did you just plan on hiding from her for a few more months?"

Emory's eyes moved from Eli, to Luna, and back again. He hadn't been coming around because he was hiding his injuries from her. He didn't want her to see him like this. He didn't want her to see him as weak or no longer in control of his Pride.

She opened her mouth to question him further, but the front door flew open and smacked her in the back.

Turning, ready to Shift to fight, she growled at Gray, Micah, and Reed, who were all shoving their way into Eli's house.

"You were taking too long," Reed said when she cocked an eyebrow at them. "Hey, Eli." Reed's eyes moved to Luna's and he growled. Luna took a step back. "Who the fuck did that to your face?" Reed asked.

Luna's hand raised and she covered the deep, silvery pink scar ruining that part of her face. She was still gorgeous, but it was obviously a sore subject for her. With one quick glance at Emory, she turned and ran up the stairs, taking them two at a time.

"Smooth, Reed," Micah muttered under his breath. Reed just shrugged.

"Dude, what happened to *you*?" Reed asked, keeping with his habit of blurting the first thing that came to his pea-sized brain.

"Could you guys give us a minute?" Emory asked, not taking her eyes off her mate as anger, lust, and concern warred within her.

"Why? So you can rip the towel off his waist and make up with him? Because, since we haven't heard you yelling and cussing yet, I assume that means he's no longer in trouble," Reed said.

"Holy shit, Reed. Can you shut your trap for, like, five minutes? Please?" Emory said, whirling on him.

Reed zipped his mouth and held his hands behind his back.

"Idiot," she whispered as she turned back to Eli.

"Problems with the Pride?" Gray asked, a soft, slight growl lacing his words.

Eli sighed heavily and ran a hand down his face. "I'll be right back." He trudged up the stairs like each step was painful and, when he came back down, he wore a pair of jeans and was pulling a t-shirt over his head.

Jerking his head, he motioned for Emory and her Pack to follow him down the hall into the kitchen. He sat at a butcher block style table, as did Emory, Reed, and Gray, but Micah remained standing, his back leaned against the wall.

"What the fuck is going on?" Gray asked.

"Why are you guys here?" Eli asked.

All eyes turned to Emory. "I thought…I haven't seen you in a few days."

"And you thought I used you for sex and dumped you," Eli finished for her.

Her cheeks burned and she averted her eyes. He looked like she'd hurt him.

"What was I supposed to think?" she said with a shrug, but she couldn't hide the deep blush of shame hot in her cheeks.

"Definitely not that," he said, pushing a hand through his hair.

"What happened, Eli? What's going on with your Pride? Why are you covered in cuts and bruises?" Emory asked.

She wanted to know who did this to him. Now that the worry he'd been trying to blow her off was over, anger took its place. She wanted to plant her fist against someone's mouth, Shift, and attack whatever asshole had the nerve to lay a finger on her mate.

Sitting up straight, she realized she fully understood Eli's anger over what Jace had done to her. It wasn't jealousy or a hit to his ego, rather a natural urge to protect his mate at all costs.

And she was ready to tear through the entire Pride to find out who'd hurt her mate.

Gray's eyes moved over to Emory and narrowed. When he looked back at Eli, she realized exactly what had grabbed his attention; the mark right there on his shoulder. They must not have noticed it when they all came barreling through the door when he was wearing nothing but a towel.

"I have a few lions reluctant to go by the new rules," Eli said, dragging a hand roughly down his jaw. There was at least three days' worth of stubble across his cheeks and chin, and it gave him an even sexier, more rugged appearance.

"I thought you kicked them all out," Emory said, her brows pulling together.

"I did. Out of the territory, but they're still technically Tammen. I've had a few Alpha challenges."

That explained the wounds covering his body.

"I take it you won them since you're still here," Gray said, crossing his arms and leaning back in his chair. Gray's eyes roamed the parts of Eli's body that could still be seen with his shirt and pants on. "The other guys better look a hell of a lot worse."

Eli snorted and nodded with a small smile.

"Is this because of me?" Emory asked, unable to hold the question in any longer.

Eli's eyes raised to hers and he just stared. The fact he didn't immediately deny it told her all she needed to know.

Emory looked at her Pack and then back at Eli. "Is there somewhere I can stay?"

"What?" Reed said, lunging to his feet.

"He literally just said there have been Alpha challenges and you want to stay here?" Micah said from behind her.

"His mate isn't staying with him. That shows weakness," Emory said, standing her ground.

"It's too dangerous, Em," Gray said, turning only his eyes to her.

"I'll be fine."

"The fuck you will. The challenges are because of the new rules. And you're a chick," Reed said, throwing his hands in the air.

"Thanks for noticing," Emory said, her brows pulled up and together as she shook her head at him.

"It's not a good idea," Eli said.

Emory turned her full attention to her mate. "Am I right? Is it because I'm not here? Is it showing weakness?"

Eli rolled his neck from side to side, a loud pop echoing through the room. Again, silence.

"That's what I thought. Would I be in danger if I stayed here?"

"That's the thing. I'm not sure. You know I'd never let anything happen to you, but we both have jobs. I won't be here twenty-four/seven."

"Has anything happened to the other lionesses since all this has been going on?" Emory asked.

Again, Eli rubbed the stubble on his jaw. The whiskers might be irritating him, but she was really digging the look.

"Not yet. Just a lot of threats."

Gray leaned forward, resting his elbows on the table. "Do you need some backup?"

Emory's head whipped around to stare at her Alpha. Was he seriously offering up help to Eli? Was he suggesting someone from Big River come hang out to give him a hand? She'd always loved and respected Gray; that love and respect grew tenfold in that moment.

Eli studied Gray. "You offering to send some of your people to help?"

"I can talk to the bears and panthers. Maybe with a few extra men, you can run the fuckers off permanently."

"Gray," Emory whispered, in total awe of her Alpha.

He glanced at her. "If one of mine is going to be staying here, I'm not taking any chances, Em. I'm not going to force you to stay away from your mate, but I'm not sure I'm comfortable having him on our land. Not yet." He looked up to Eli, but there was no hate or anger like she usually saw aimed at him. "Will that keep her safe?"

One of Eli's shoulders raised slightly. "Wouldn't hurt."

"Do you want me here?" Emory asked softly, her eyes on Eli only.

He stared at her, lust, affection, and something else bright in his eyes. "You should know that answer by now."

She ducked his gaze as warmth filled her chest. She'd thought she'd just wanted to date for a while and get to know each other. But the last five days without seeing him, without feeling his hands on her face, her back, or any part of her body were damn near painful. She hated it and she struggled with her wolf every day. She wasn't used to having to keep her animal calm. She'd never had any problems with losing control before. She'd never understood why it was so hard for people like Micah.

But now? Yeah, she fully understood how hard it was to keep a restless animal in her skin.

"I'll get my stuff and be back by morning."

She stood and looked at her Pack expectantly. For some reason, she thought this would be one of those uber dramatic scenes like in a TV show or movie where they all nodded resolutely, climbed to their feet, and ushered her back to pack her belongings.

Instead, they all stared at her like she'd lost her ever loving mind.

"We've got a few more things to figure out before we go pack your makeup, Em," Micah teased.

She turned and stuck her tongue out at him, then hid her smile as she lowered back into her seat.

"I'll talk to Aron and Carter and get them on board," Gray said.

"You sure this is a good idea?" Micah said, his voice deep and growly.

Emory knew Micah didn't like being in Tammen's area and held a lot of resentment for how Callie was treated. But the main culprit was dead. The former Alpha was dead. And it seemed Eli was steadily exiling members who thought too much like Rhett.

It wasn't the same Pride, even if there were still some who preferred things the way they used to be.

"No. But if she's set on staying here, what other option do I have?"

"We could just carry her back kicking and screaming," Reed said.

Now, Emory was fully aware Reed was kidding. He even held his hands out when Emory shot him a glare. Eli, however, was still in full fight mode.

"Touch her and fucking die," Eli said, his voice no longer human.

"Dude, I was playing. And I'm pretty sure Emory would kick your ass if you marred my gorgeous face," Reed said, his head snapping back in surprise.

"He's joking, Eli. Chill out," Emory said, smiling and shaking her head at Reed. Leave it to him to joke at the wrong time.

Eli still trembled, his eyes were bright gold, but he forced a smile, as if both sides of him were warring each other to pummel Reed. Emory would never let that happen. Neither would the rest of the guys. She just appreciated that he was able to reign himself in before he did anything stupid.

"Back to the subject at hand," Emory said, raising a brow at Reed. "I'm staying here. I'm coming back tomorrow morning. Period." She leveled a gaze on each of the guys and they nodded, although the looks on their faces let her know exactly what they thought of the idea.

None of them, including Eli, liked the thought of her there when everyone was fighting the Alpha.

Something else they'd yet to figure out. "Where the hell am I going to sleep?"

She knew all the rooms were already taken, and she wasn't about to kick anyone out of their beds or throw them out. It wasn't her place and she wasn't that kind of person.

"You can have the couch while we're figuring this out. I still—"

"I get it. You don't like it. It's happening, so we need to figure out logistics."

"Where the hell will the other guys stay?" Reed asked.

"They'll want to stay wherever Em is, so they'll just crash on the floor. How many women do you have staying here?" Gray asked.

"Three. My sister and two others who left their mates," Eli said.

"Either of those men the ones giving you problems?" Gray asked.

"One. They were both sold to the same man. And, yeah, he's one of the main culprits. Kicked him out last night after he lost."

Gray smirked. "Hope the fucker was bleeding when he left."

"He was limping," Eli said, returning the smirk.

Gray surprised the shit out of Emory when he reached across the table and held his fist out to Eli, who bumped it with his own.

"Colton will probably volunteer," Micah said.

"I don't think that's a good idea," Emory said. After what happened to his dad within the territory, he'd come in with a chip on his shoulder. She wanted whoever hung out to be objective. She needed a more neutral party there.

"If he wants to be here, I'm not going to stop him," Gray said, raising one brow at her.

"Is this going to cause more problems, Eli?" Emory asked.

They were making plans for his Pride without truly asking his input. She knew the reason her Pack was doing it and it really had nothing to do with Eli or the lions. They were doing it to protect Emory when Eli wasn't around.

He shrugged again. "Might. Or it might show an alliance. We'll find out, I guess."

His eyes snagged Emory's and she could tell he was apprehensive about having outsiders there, but there was definite happiness. He was excited he was going to have his mate within touching distance instead of this phone dating they'd been doing.

After the plans were laid, Emory left with her Pack to gather the things she'd need for a while. She wasn't exactly planning on moving in with Eli. This was to show his Pride he hadn't lost control. It was to show them his lion had not only claimed Emory, but won her over to his side. She hated that he had to show dominance over a female to earn their respect, but they had no idea what kind of woman she really was.

But they were going to find out real soon.

Chapter Nine

Emory stood in the middle of her living room and looked around. It was so tiny, but it was hers. It had been her home for years. And now, she was leaving it to go bunk with three other females and her mate. She'd go from having her own space to sleeping on the couch with her mate either squeezing in with her or sleeping on the floor.

With whoever volunteered to hang out until all the crap was cleared up with Tammen.

She'd thought her living quarters were tight before, it was about to get downright claustrophobic. At least two large male Shifters and four females, all fighting for one shower and two toilets. At least she'd never been a female who spent much time getting ready. All she needed was some soap and clean clothes and she was good to go.

"You ready, Em?" Reed called from her front porch.

Grabbing a couple of duffel bags she'd borrowed from the rest of the Pack and hitching them over her shoulder, she nodded and smiled as she left her home for a while. Well, she hoped it was only for a while. She wasn't sure she could leave her little sanctuary and her Pack forever.

Emory stepped onto the porch and pulled her door closed behind her. "Yeah. I think."

"You can change your mind, you know. You don't have to do this."

"Yes, I do."

Emory glanced over to the vehicles and smiled as she shook her heard. Every single member of her Pack stood in front of the trucks and cars, sad looks on their faces. Callie and Nova were both openly crying while Gray and Micah stood with their arms crossed and eyes on the ground.

Tristan had a bag over his shoulder, as well.

"Take it you're coming tonight?" she asked him. He just nodded, turned his back to her, and tossed his bag into the cab of his truck.

"Me, too," Reed said. "Bag's already in Tristan's truck."

"Holy crap. Are you actually letting someone else drive for once?" she teased. He didn't smile or tease back. "Guys. I'm literally going to be less than ten minutes away. I'm not going to be gone forever."

"Why can't he just come here?" Nova said with a sniffle.

"Well, for one, he can't fix his Pride if he's here. And two…talk to your mate about that one." She winked at Gray, but just like Reed, he didn't return her happiness or excitement.

She was just as worried as them, but this could be a really good thing. Not only was it a step for all of them to start healing, but it was a way to bring the Prides, Pack, and Clan together. It would be a rocky alliance, but it was just the beginning to what could be some really great things.

"I'm going to miss you so much," Nova said, rushing Emory and throwing her arms around her. She sobbed softly.

"Nova, seriously. I'm still going to be coming around. I'll probably see you almost every day."

"It's not the same and you know it. How long will it be before you even find out whether I left another present in your house?"

"I'm sure I'll find it the next time I'm here, which will probably be *every day*. I'm just on the other side of the woods. Stop being so girly." Emory chuckled and pulled out of Nova's arms.

Callie hugged her next. She didn't beg her to stay, didn't complain about her not being two houses down. When she pulled back, the tears were streaming down her face. "Please be careful," she pleaded.

"I'll be fine. You guys, oh my gosh. I should take a picture of your faces."

"To remember us by?" Nova said as another tear rolled down her face.

"No. So you can see how ridiculous you all look."

Emory shook her head as she headed to her own car. She wouldn't bother mentioning how her stomach was in knots or her legs felt like jelly. She wouldn't tell them she really didn't want to go or how terrified she really was. She didn't even want to admit all that to herself.

"I'll text you guys when I get settled in, okay?" she said as she pulled her car door open. "Love you guys."

Even though she'd made fun of them for their pity party, she took an extra moment to soak in their faces. She just prayed she could keep her promise about returning to them and this wouldn't turn into some suicide mission.

Her knee bounced all the way to Eli's. She received glares from a couple people as she navigated through the little village they called home, but mostly she just got a lot of curious looks from lionesses and a few males.

Eli was waiting out front when she pulled into the driveway and parked behind his Mustang. Her little Audi was so out of place amongst all the muscle cars lined up along the street.

"Hey," he called out when she climbed from her front seat.

He was beside her and taking her bags from her hands before she had a chance to pull them over her shoulder. "Luna's been pacing like a fool while waiting for you to get here," he said with a wide smile.

He looked over Emory's shoulder and nodded to Reed and Tristan, then led them all inside.

And, as he'd said, Luna was waiting in the front room, her arms wrapped around her waist. "Are you seriously coming to stay?" she asked, her voice holding a slight tremor. Was she afraid of Emory? Of her friends standing behind her?

When Emory nodded, Luna crossed the room and hugged her tightly. Too tightly. The air rushed out of her lungs as Luna's arms tightened like a freaking boa constrictor.

"Thank you," she whispered against her ear.

Luna pulled back and quickly swiped a tear from under her eye.

"For what? Crowding you guys some more?" she teased.

Maybe she was more like Reed than she realized. Because her first thought was to diffuse the tension with a little humor.

No one laughed.

"You being here is big, Emory. They'll have to show him some respect now."

Emory looked from Luna to Eli then back. It was obvious Luna loved her brother. It was also obvious she was broken in so many ways if she thought Emory's mere presence was going to change things any time soon.

Luna took Emory for a quick tour, pointing out the bedrooms upstairs and introducing her to the two other women she'd be living with. They were friendly but extremely closed off. They'd only just been freed from a form of slavery a few months back. It would take them a long time to heal from that.

Hell. Emory had been free for years and she still struggled with it sometimes.

She found the bathroom with the only shower, then rejoined the guys downstairs. They sat at a table, beers in front of them, but no one was talking or even looking at each other. Great. This was going to be a long day and it had only just started.

****

The second Eli heard Emory's little car coming close, his lion immediately sat up and went into fight mode. He searched the faces of the Pride members watching her entry and catalogued who he'd need to meet with later. And by meet with, he meant threaten and possibly beat the piss out of them.

Even the two males from her Pack who'd joined her had him on edge. It was like there was this constant need to shadow her, to tuck her under his arm and guard her from the outside world. He could tell she was nervous by the giggles and the way she had a hard time making eye contact with anyone for longer than a second at a time. His mate never backed down from anyone and never had a problem looking someone in the eye. Her discomfort made it all even harder.

Why had he agreed to this? Even with the extra hands and eyes to keep her safe, he wanted to murder every male in his Pride who'd ever accepted a mate against her will.

And now she was going to have to sleep on his couch because he didn't have anymore bedrooms. All three women had offered up their beds, but Emory refused to take them. She'd said the couch was fine. What kind of mate and Alpha was he if he couldn't at least provide a comfortable sleeping arrangement?

"I should get an air mattress," he blurted out as Emory and Luna discussed going to the grocery store and having some kind of introductory cookout.

"What?" Emory asked, confusion making her dark brows shoot high.

"For you to sleep on."

"Being as your living room isn't exactly giant, we'd all have to squeeze on that thing."

"You could sleep upstairs with the girls," Eli said.

"Mate," she said, crossing the room and stopping his heart with that one word. Her hand landed on his jaw and her thumb rasped against the stubble. Why hadn't he at least shaved before she'd gotten there?

Because you were too busy warning everyone and fighting all night.

"The couch is fine. Shoot, the floor is fine. It's just until we get everything settled. Then, as houses open, the girls can get their own places."

Oh, that sounded so fucking good. He loved the thought of the lionesses in his Pride safe enough to live alone. He liked the idea of being alone with his mate even better. And he really loved the fact she was making plans to bring his Pride together, regardless of the fear he could feel pouring from her in waves.

"I don't think a lot of the guys will come," Luna said, picking the conversation right back up and turning her back on Eli with a frown.

Luna wasn't at ease around anyone but him. Yet, there she was, making plans with Emory to get the whole Pride gathered in one place. She even smiled and laughed a little. It was the most joy he'd seen from her since they were kids. She wasn't even hiding from the Big River guys.

Maybe Emory and her Pack *was* going to be a good influence on his people.

Eli looked at Reed and Tristan with his brows to his hairline when Emory demanded someone make a run for more lawn chairs.

"What? You don't have enough for a good cookout," she said, propping her hands on her hips.

"Dude, don't look at us. She and Nova pull this shit on us all the time," Reed said.

"Oh, whatever. I don't remember hearing anyone complain."

"Not complaining. Just saying. This isn't the Pack or even the Clan, Em. Good luck getting those bastards to show up." Reed looked over at Eli. "No offense, man."

Eli raised both hands and shook his head. None taken. Some of the guys there *were* bastards. And Reed was right; his people weren't like hers. Even if some of them showed up, he already knew how it was going to go. Someone would end up making a comment about Emory and Eli, Tristan, and Reed would get bent out of shape and there was sure to be at least one fight.

A dull throb started behind his eyes. He wrapped his hand around his forehead and massaged his temples to no avail. Until he knew without a doubt that his mate and sister were safe, that fucking headache wasn't going anywhere.

"You sure today is good? It was hard enough before you got here," Eli said, his hand still wrapped around his forehead.

"It was hard because I wasn't here. These assholes need to see me. They need to see how a woman is supposed to be treated. And they need to see you've got a big ass team behind you if they want to continue being jackoffs," Emory said.

Reed and Eli snorted. Tristan shook his head. She was a trip. Even though she was scared, she was still determined to make everything right. They might be new to mated life, but it was obvious she was already seeing his people as her people. She didn't know them. Had only briefly met the two women cowering upstairs, but she was ready to put it all out there to make life better for everyone.

And he knew she'd throw down the gauntlet to anyone who refused to cooperate with her plans.

"Should we invite the bears?" Emory suddenly asked.

"No," all three men answered in unison.

"One thing at a time, Em," Reed said.

"Let's see if we can get through the night without any bloodshed," Eli said.

"Stupid idea," Tristan muttered under his breath. The man rarely talked, but this was one of those times Eli fully agreed with him.

All he could do was support Emory's wishes and pray to whoever was listening that everyone was still standing at the end of the night and no one was stupid enough to fuck with his mate or sister.

****

Emory made Reed go with her and Luna into town to buy supplies. She left the invites to Eli, who growled a human sound of frustration before kissing her and swatting her on the ass as she walked to her car.

For some reason, him slapping her ass made her feel at home rather than put off by the manly show of affection. Even if they were new to this, she knew him. How could she have thought he'd throw her away so easily after everything they'd been through together? Even the act of him claiming her when Deathport called dibs could've caused a huge riff in his uneasy partnership with the wolves.

Now that Rhett and Anson were both dead, neither of them gave two shits what Deathport thought of their union. In a strange way, though, she was kind of thankful for their obsession with her. It brought Eli straight to her.

Luna and Emory filled up two carts with Reed complaining the whole way, then headed home with a ton of meat, chips, and beer. She didn't bother with anything like cole slaw and potato salad. She wanted something simple for their first time hanging out.

"Does anyone own a grill?" Emory asked as they got close to a hardware store.

"Yeah. The old guy who owns Dodson's does. I'm sure he won't mind us borrowing it," Luna answered. "Can I borrow your phone?"

Emory frowned back at her from the front seat of Reed's truck. "You don't have one?"

"Nope. I think Callie was the first lioness to get one and that was only after she joined you guys."

"Well, damn. Guess we're going to have to get you one before I leave," Emory said, turning back in her seat.

When Luna didn't say anything else, Emory turned back around to see her blonde brows low. "What?"

"Do you have to leave?"

"I mean, eventually. I can't sleep on the couch forever, Luna."

She just met this woman, yet she liked her already. Emory could see so much of herself in the woman. Luna just had to find her inner strength again.

"It's just…you could be really good for the Pride."

"It's not her job to fix your people," Reed said, glancing at her in the rearview mirror.

"They're my people now, too," Emory said, surprising herself as much as Reed, who gaped at her from behind the wheel.

She'd fight for Eli and Luna and the lionesses until her last breath. She might be new to mated life. She might be out of her element in a Pride full of lions, but if they were Eli's people, that made them her people, too. And damn it, she needed everything to level out so the women here could live a normal life. Even if that meant some of the males would have to leave the Pride permanently.

"Whatever. I still don't think you should be here," Reed said, draping his wrist over the wheel as they cruised down the highway.

"You scared you're going to have to fight a lion?" Emory teased.

Reed snorted and shook his head. She knew damn well he could hold his own. She'd witnessed it when they'd fought the Pride and the wolves. But she had to bust his balls. At least a little.

There was a small crowd gathered in front of Eli's and when a few bodies shuffled to the side, Emory jumped from the truck before it was fully stopped.

"Emory, wait! Fuck," Reed barked out as she ran headfirst into a faceoff.

Eli was nose to nose with a male as big as him. Like a fool, she tried to wedge herself between them just to be yanked back. Turning on whoever had the balls to touch her, she snarled at Tristan.

"Stay back," he said, his eyes bright blue.

"They're fucking wolves, asshole!" the guy yelled at Eli, lifting his hand and pointing at where Reed now flanked Emory's other side.

"And she's my fucking mate. You got a problem with that? Bye, dickhead."

"You'd pick her over your Pride?"

Eli turned and looked at each person standing there watching. "Listen to me now. Emory is a part of this Pride. She is my mate and has chosen to live within our territory. If one of you mother fuckers so much as blinks wrong in her direction, you'll answer to me."

"And to her Pack," Reed said, crossing his arms over his chest. He instantly went from that playful guy to full on badass in a blink of an eye.

"She's a female," the guy said.

"She, as well as every lioness in this Pride, is an equal. Again, you got a problem with that..." Eli jerked his head toward the street, telling him to hit the road.

"Fuck you." The guy spit on the ground at Eli's feet and stomped away, giving Eli his back in a show of disrespect.

Eli could've beat his ass and made an example of him. Instead, he studied the rest of the Pride, looking each person in the eye, his golden gaze bright as his body trembled and the scent of fur was suffocating.

"Anyone else?"

"Did you just kick him out?" a female asked from Emory's left. She glanced over at her; the woman stuck out from the rest of her people with her fancy clothes and perfectly highlighted hair.

"I gave him the option. Same option I'm giving the rest of you. Females are not your fucking possessions. My mate is not a fucking possession. The wolves are our guests and will be treated as such as long as they're here."

"Are they her bodyguards or something?" the fancy woman asked.

"They're my family," Emory said, speaking up for herself.

Eli turned his full body to stare down at her and nodded.

"This isn't how it has to be, guys. We can be a family, too. Whatever the hell your parents fed you your whole life is a lie. Women aren't just baby makers and you guys?" Emory huffed out a laugh. "You guys are worth more than breeding females and muscles."

Someone snorted, but a few women actually nodded in agreement, their eyes wide as Emory spoke.

"I'm here now. I'm with my mate. And, yeah, big deal, I'm a wolf." Emory held her arms out to her sides. "The Second in our Pack is mated to one of your lionesses." More nods from the females. One of the guys looked curious, but not quite as convinced as the women. Well, the women except Fancy Pants, who was glaring at her with her thin arms crossed over her chest.

"Are all of you staying?" a guy asked from the back of the crowd.

"No. My Pack will go home once I feel safe."

"Why are you even here if you don't want to be?" Fancy Pants asked.

Emory didn't know the woman, didn't know her name, and already she didn't like her. "Because this is where I belong."

"You belong in Big River," the woman said.

"I belong with my mate. And guess what, just like with that asshole," Emory said, pointing in the direction of the guy who'd stormed off, "you don't have to like it and you don't have to stay here."

That earned snorts from a few of the women who'd previously agreed with her.

Fancy Pants smirked and looked at the other females. "Yeah. Because we have choices." She turned on her way-too-high-for-the-occasion heels and left the rest of them standing there.

"Well then. Great first impression, huh?" Emory said, turning to look up at Eli.

He was smiling down at her, shaking his head. It seemed she caused the same reaction from everyone lately.

After a tense half hour, Eli fired up the grill and let Reed take over when he started burning the hot dogs.

"How does a man not know how to grill fucking hot dogs?" Reed mumbled to himself as he tried to salvage the meal.

Most of the crowd stuck around, milling around without really saying much. No one had bought chairs, even after she tried to guilt trip her Pack guys and Eli, so Emory took it upon herself to go inside and bring out a few chairs from the kitchen.

Two women smiled widely and went into their own houses, returning with mismatched chairs and setting them beside Emory's. It was still tense, but the mood was changing. This was something none of them had ever had. This was a new experience for them all. While some might have been reluctant, it was obvious it was needed by the rest.

After a while, a few of the women loosened up, even drank a beer or two, and started talking to Emory. One of them even attempted a conversation with Tristan, but when he gave her his usual one or two word answers, she gave up with a sad look in her eyes.

"It's not you. He's super shy," Emory whispered, leaning over and getting right in the woman's bubble.

The woman smiled over at Tristan as if they were telling secrets and nodded her head. When the woman looked away, Emory widened her eyes and shook her head at him. If he refused to talk to anyone for fear of being judged, he'd never find his mate. And she desperately wanted that for him. They'd talked enough when they were on their own to know he wanted not just a mate, but kids someday. She couldn't picture him as a dad, but only because he never talked. How was he supposed to woo a woman or correct his child if he never opened his damn mouth?

As much as she wanted to push him, she had her own issues, like the fact Fancy Pants was back and glaring at her. She hadn't brought a chair with her and wasn't sitting on the ground. Of course she wasn't. She might get her pretty, expensive clothes dirty if she did that.

Realizing how bitchy she sounded in her head about a woman she knew literally nothing of other than the way she looked, she turned her attention to the other women finally talking openly. They were smiling and joking, and didn't even retreat into themselves when Reed or Eli spoke to them.

With the exception of the guy who'd bitched about the wolves being there and the occasional glare, she'd chalk that night up to a complete success.

****

Emory had been in Tammen Pride territory for a full week. Tristan and Reed ended up taking turns after the second night instead of both of them staying. Things had been quiet and Emory just didn't think they were both needed.

Even Eli was relaxing more in the past few days since there'd been no more challenges of his authority and no more bitching about Emory or any of her Pack. At least not when she was around. She couldn't care less what they said behind her back; their opinion was none of her business.

It was time for Eli to return to work. Emory had gone back yesterday after taking a few sick days to get situated. She wanted to make sure everyone saw her and knew exactly who she was and that she wasn't some pushover or broken lioness.

And speaking of broken lionesses, Luna was more than coming out of her shell. She and Reed had gotten into it a few times, but it was over benign crap like who was spending too long in the bathroom, or the fact Reed had a habit of leaving the toilet seat up.

Eli had been shocked speechless when his sister had not only stood up for herself, but called Reed a few colorful names.

"You're good for her," he said, pulling her close.

Of course, that was about as much affection as she'd gotten since she'd been there. They were never alone. Never. There was always someone in the house, someone riding along with them to the store, someone vying for his attention. It had been far too long since she'd felt Eli's body pressed against hers, even in just a nice, long hug, that she was getting cranky. It appeared she'd become addicted to her mate.

Emory stood on the front porch and waved Eli off as he followed the old guy, Chuck, to the garage. He'd been worried, but she was never alone. To her utter surprise, the bears declared they wanted a chance to stay with Emory. It had been an option when they'd discussed her coming there, but she still wasn't sure it was the greatest idea.

As Eli's Mustang rounded the corner, Colton's big F-350 came into view. Well, shit. Of all the bears, it was going to be the one who would have the most against the Pride. Straightening her shoulders, she fastened a smile on her face and waited for Colton to make his way up the driveway to her.

"Why are you grimacing?" Colton asked, looking her over, probably for wounds.

"What? I was smiling...shut up. Come on in." She led him inside and into the kitchen where Reed was currently eating a bowl of kids' cereal.

"What's up, man?" Reed asked around a mouthful of Frooty Pebbles.

Colton leaned over the table and bumped fists with Reed, then straightened. "Where's everyone else?"

"Eli just left," Emory said.

"Yeah. I passed him. I was told there would be chicks here."

"There are women, yeah," Luna said, walking in and freezing when she spotted Colton, her eyes going wide.

Well, so much for getting over some of her fear.

Emory could understand, though. Colton was as wide as the doorway and stood just about as tall. Luna had no idea he was one of the sweetest and kindest men she ever met. All she saw was a behemoth staring at her with intense blue eyes and a week's worth of copper stubble.

"What's with the beard?" Emory asked, pulling the attention back to her. She hated being in the spotlight, but anything was better than watching Luna shrink before her very eyes.

Colton grinned and stroked his impressive whiskers. "You like it? I figured I could save myself some money on razors if I just stopped shaving for a while."

"Hm. I should try that," Emory said.

"Please don't. Beards on women are not sexy," Reed said.

Emory grabbed a towel and tossed it at his face. He dodged to the side and laughed openly, showing the room his mouthful of rainbow-colored mush.

"Gross. Close your mouth."

Luna backed from the room silently, her eyes never leaving Colton's back. Poor girl. It had taken Emory years, and it would probably take Luna just as long. The damage didn't happen overnight; it wouldn't heal overnight, either.

"What are you planning today?" Colton asked, pulling out a chair and sitting as if he'd been to Eli's a dozen times.

"I've got some errands to run and I want to get some more food. And some…toiletries."

"Are you getting tampons or condoms?" Reed asked, then threw his hand out. "You know what? Never mind. I don't want to know either way."

"There are four women living under one roof, Reed. And then there's always one of you. When would I put condoms to use?"

Reed made a gagging sound. "Dude. No one wants to think of their sister having sex."

Emory shook her head as she left the room to grab her purse. Luna planned to go with her, but when Emory went to find her, the door was locked.

"Luna? You ready to go?"

"Hold on," Luna called back through the closed door.

Emory leaned against the wall across from the room and waited. Two minutes later, the door opened and Luna stepped out, her purse over her shoulder. And a lot of makeup covering the scar on her face.

Instead of mentioning it, she smiled and led the way down the stairs. Only one week, and the place felt like home. The other girls, Petra and Amber, had finally started to confide in her and told her about their time with Tammen. It woke up some of those old fears she'd originally had about coming to the territory, but she reminded herself those jackasses weren't just gone, but some were dead.

Even though they were starting to open up, they refused to spend too much time around any of her friends. She didn't blame them. Just like Luna, it would take a lot of work and time to heal wounds unseen by the eye.

Luna didn't even look in Colton's direction as they left the house, just hurried out the front door as Emory told Colton and Reed goodbye. Reed was heading to work that day and would go back home that night. He asked her if she wanted him to stop by, just in case, but she was fine. Things were smooth sailing…kind of.

"Why is the bear here?" Luna asked once they were in the car and on the way to the store.

"I guess it's his day off. They're all taking turns."

"Yeah, but why that bear? He hates us," Luna said with her arms crossed over her chest and her bottom lip poking out a little.

"He hates Rhett. Rhett's dead. End of story."

Well, she hoped that was the end of the story. She hadn't really had a chance to talk to Colton about all this and she just hoped he could contain his anger when he was around Eli or the other males. She had no worries about him around the lionesses; just like every single member of her family, her friends would never hurt a female. Ever.

The rest of their trip was in relative silence. Luna had closed herself off and closed Emory out. Emory loved Colton and was glad he was there, but maybe it wasn't such a great idea. She wanted the females, *all* the females to feel empowered while she was staying as safe as possible. Although, no one had even looked at her cross-eyed in two days. Eli's warning had worked.

That didn't mean she was naïve enough to believe they were totally in the clear. Not yet, anyway.

When things settled, then what? Where would she go? Would she go back home? She missed her people and had totally broken her promise and hadn't been back home since she'd left. But she ached for Eli when they were apart. Already, she missed him and it hadn't been two hours since he'd left for work. She still had another six or more to go before he'd come ambling into the house, covered in grease and smelling like exhaust and diesel fuel.

Emory pulled her car into the driveway and began unloading the grocery bags from the backseat. A large hand reached over her shoulder to grab one and Emory turned to thank Colton for his help. Only, it wasn't Colton.

"I've got it," the guy said, a grin on his face.

She'd seen him around but hadn't really talked to him. He'd been one of the guys who'd glared at her when she'd arrived and didn't bother coming to their little get together. She hadn't seen him since. As far as she knew, he was complying like he was supposed to.

"How you been, Emory?" he asked.

She frowned up at him. "Uh, good. Thanks."

How had she been? She'd been there for a week and this was the first time he'd bother to talk to his Alpha's mate and that was what he came up with? He had to be trying to suck up or something.

Luna eyed him and stepped to stand beside Emory. That made her nervous. Or maybe it was Luna's nervous energy putting her on edge. Either way, she instinctually took a step back so this guy was no longer in her personal space.

"I'm Brian," he said, shifting three bags onto one arm to offer his hand.

Emory stared at it like she was ready for it to morph into a snake and bite her. Finally, she slipped her hand into his, squeezed once, then pulled back and fought the urge to wipe her palm on her shorts. He was sweaty and gross. And he was creeping her out the way he was looking at her.

He could've just been trying to be friendly, but she was getting bad mojo from him and wanted him away from her. Like, immediately.

Brian followed them into the house with the bags dangling from his fingers. When he spotted Colton standing in the kitchen, his tree trunk arms crossed over his chest, he lost a little of his machismo.

"Colton," he said, offering his hand.

Emory had to press her lips into a thin line as Brian stared at Colton's massive paw the way she'd stared at his hand–like he was scared it would bite him.

Setting the bags at his feet, Brian shook Colton's hand and she didn't miss the way he pumped his hand as if Colton had squeezed too hard. She had to turn her back when the smile broke free. If Brian was trying to make amends or whatever, she didn't want to ruin it by laughing in his face.

"It was good to see you, Emory," Brian said.

She turned and he was staring at her, his brows pinched together in anger. Well, what the hell had she done to piss him off? Nothing. Just because Colton didn't know his strength didn't mean he needed to give her the stink eye.

When the door opened and closed hard enough to rattle windows, Colton turned to Emory. "Who was that douche?"

Emory shrugged. "Brian," she answered.

"Stay away from him. He's a pig," Luna said with her back to the room as she unpacked groceries.

Once the bags were empty, Luna excused herself and jogged up the stairs like she couldn't get away from Colton fast enough.

"Dude. You freaked her out," Emory said.

"What? I didn't say a word to her," Colton said, his hands out, his eyes wide and his brows to his hairline.

Emory swept her hands up and down in the air, indicating his size. "You're like a damn giant and you're standing there all intimidating. You could've at least smiled at her or something."

Colton still looked confused as he looked up at the ceiling like he was looking for her. "Should I go say something to her?"

"No. Absolutely not. Just...I don't know. Be quiet and soft or whatever."

He snorted, then sucked his lips into his mouth when she glared.

"Dork," she said as she passed him.

She plopped down on the couch and pulled her phone out to text Eli. It was clingy but she didn't care. She shot him a quick text, just telling him she missed him and was thinking about him, then hugged the phone to her chest until it dinged.

I love you.

Emory stared down at the phone. What the...They hadn't exchanged those words yet. And she hadn't heard him say it to Luna so it wasn't some habit. Was he really telling her that over a text?

No privacy. They'd had zero privacy since she'd gotten there. He hadn't had a chance to tell her. And this was his way. What should she type back? Her fingers shook as she held them over the phone, unsure of whether to say it back or ditto or just leave that hanging in the air.

Instead of any of those, she sent back a heart emoji and hit send. Holy crap. Their relationship just went to the next level. Over text. Not exactly romantic, but she still couldn't help the mushy smile as she dropped back onto the cushions and laid staring at the ceiling.

Once everything was settled, there was no way she'd stay in this house. Not with everyone else. Either he'd have to come back to the Pack with her or they were getting their own place. Because she wasn't sure how much more patience she had.

Chapter Ten

Eli and Emory snuggled on the couch while Colton rolled onto his side and pulled a pillow over his head.

"He didn't really say anything. Just gives me the creeps," Emory said, telling him all about her encounter with Brian.

"He was a douche," Colton said, his voice muffled by the pillow.

"You can roll over, Colton. Not like we're going to get naked with you lying right there," Emory said through a chuckle.

He flopped onto his back like he was throwing a tantrum. "Yeah, but I still have to listen to you whisper sweet nothings."

Eli and Emory both chuckled. "You can hear us whether you cover your head or not. Stop being a child."

Colton actually rolled his eyes at Emory. "That dick acted like he knew Em."

Eli looked down at Emory. "What did he say, exactly?"

"When he was outside, he asked how I've been. In here, he said it was good to see me. I've never said a word to him before today."

Eli looked over Emory's head at the far wall as he chewed the inside of his cheek. "I'll talk to him. Tell him to stay away from you."

"Don't do that. He didn't do anything. He was probably just nervous and didn't know what to say."

"He's a douche," Colton repeated.

"Got it, Colton. You're not a fan."

She loved how easy his being there was already. He wasn't holding his father's murder against Eli. There was no lingering grudge or price to be paid in blood. He was just there as her friend, making sure she was safe. He and Eli actually got along pretty well, even if most of their conversations were in one-word sentences and grunts.

"I'm just saying, I'd stay away from his dumb ass." Colton pushed up onto one elbow. "Want me to scare the shit out of him?" he asked through a huge smile.

"Colton!" Emory whisper-screamed and tossed a pillow at him.

He caught it mid-air and tucked it under his head. "Thanks."

"If he scares you, I'll talk to him," Eli said when they'd quieted down.

"No." Emory shook her head and then laid back against his chest. "Just leave it alone. I don't want any extra attention. It's bad enough literally every single person here stares at me the second I step outside. I don't want them to hate me more than they already do."

"No one hates you," Eli said, pressing a kiss to her temple.

Emory snorted. "Fancy Pants does. And a few of the guys definitely hold no love for me." And she was pretty sure that was thanks to her bodyguards staying with her.

"Fancy Pants?" he asked, pulling back to look into her face.

"Yeah. The chick with the designer clothes. The prissy blonde one."

"Shawnee?"

She shrugged against his side. "I guess so. She gives me the side-eye every chance she gets."

"She's not uber friendly. That's one of Rhett's mates."

"Ohhh. That makes sense, then. She was already nuts to begin with."

Eli's chuckle was deep against her ear as it rumbled through her chest. As she listened to his heart thumping, his text came to mind. And now, she couldn't even ask him about it. Not with Colton lying there, hanging on every word.

"Hey, I was thinking," Emory said, turning so she was almost completely lying on top of Eli's big body. "We need our own place."

"Yes; you do," Colton agreed, rolling over again so his back was to them.

"What he said," Emory said, pointing at Colton.

"I know."

"I know you don't want to leave Tammen, but we've got to figure something out. Maybe the guys could start bunking together and let the girls have their houses."

"It's been hard enough getting the women out," Eli said, his eyes on the ceiling as he listened to Emory.

"Or, we could spend some time at my house."

He turned and looked down at her, his eyes so pretty as the moon glowed through the front window and cast them in a strange silvery light. They were almost translucent this way and she found herself sitting up to stare into them.

"I can't leave them, Em. Not yet."

"I need you," she whispered, glancing at Colton quickly before turning her eyes back to her mate. "Bad," she whispered even softer.

She felt him grow hard beneath her as her meaning became clear. A frustrated growl rattled up his chest and his eyes rolled closed.

"Say that again," he whispered.

"I need you," she said, bending forward to breathe the words into his ear.

He gripped the back of her head and brought her mouth down to his. They weren't kissing for ten seconds when Colton groaned.

"Oh, come on!" he said, gripping a pillow tightly to the side of his head.

Pulling away, Emory rested her forehead against Eli's. "Just think about it."

His hips pushed up against her as his nostrils flared. Well, at least she knew he was as sexually frustrated as she was.

Two more days passed and she was getting cranky. Every time he got in the shower, all Emory wanted to do was join him and lick every drop of water from his bare skin. She knew it wouldn't be frowned upon, since he was her mate. She also knew anything and everything they did would be heard by every person in the house. It might be natural for them to share their bodies, but she'd never been much into voyeurism.

"I'll be home a little after seven," Eli said, his deep voice rumbling through her phone as Emory held it between her cheek and shoulder.

"That's fine. I think I'm going to go buy some plants for your yard if that's okay."

"Why wouldn't it be? It's your home, too."

Emory was quiet for a minute. "Have you thought about what we talked about?" she finally got the courage to ask.

His heavy sigh blew through the line. "Yeah. We'll figure something out. I'm tired of jerking off in the shower when you're right downstairs."

"Perv!" she teased. Shit. Why hadn't she thought about that? All this time she'd been suffering and she could've just taken a long bath. But the real thing was so much better. Lowering her voice, she turned and looked out the window. "You really think about me in the shower?"

"Hmm…I think about that night in the woods."

"Dude, we can hear every word you're saying," someone yelled in the background.

Emory's face got hot and she covered her eyes with her hand. "Go back to work before you get in trouble."

"I told you—"

"You're the Alpha," she finished for him. "I miss you," she said before they could hang up.

"I miss you, too," he said and then ended the call.

She was surprised, even with no privacy, that he hadn't brought up his text a few days ago. And she was glad. She felt strongly for him, was falling for him like crazy, but she wasn't sure she had the courage to say the words. She didn't want to see the disappointment on his face when she didn't say it back.

"Was that Eli?" Luna's voice broke Emory out of her thoughts.

"Yeah," Emory said, shoving her phone into her back pocket. "He said he'll be home sometime after seven."

"Did you tell him about Brian?"

This was the first time Luna had wandered out of her room longer than the time it took to eat since Colton had come and gone. It was Luke's turn, and, for some reason, she didn't seem as nervous around him.

"Yeah. A couple of nights ago."

"What did he say?"

Emory shrugged. "Said he'd talk to him, but I told him to let it go. Not worth causing problems over. He was just being friendly." Emory grabbed her purse. "I'm heading into town for some flowers or something for the front yard. You want to join?"

Luna chewed on her bottom lip and looked behind her toward the kitchen where Luke was hanging out.

"Oh, come on. You haven't left the house in days. You need some fresh air."

"Fine. Let me go put on my makeup."

Emory set her bag down and took a seat. It would take Luna a few minutes to cover the scar. And Emory knew that was exactly what she meant by putting on makeup. She only wore foundation, coverup, and mascara. Someday. Emory hoped someday Luna would learn to love herself, scars and all. She hoped someday Luna would see her scars the way Emory saw hers–proof that she'd been through hell and survived.

When Luna finally came back down carrying her purse, ten minutes had passed. Not bad considering the scars were almost invisible.

As they walked through the front door, yelling to Luke where they were headed, Emory glanced at Luna over her shoulder. "Someday, you'll have to give me a makeup lesson."

"Oh, please." Luna snorted as she climbed into the passenger seat. "Like you need makeup."

"Everybody looks a little better with color," Emory repeated the line she'd heard through her life.

As Emory began to back out, Brian stepped right behind her car. "Are you trying to get run over?" Emory called through her open window.

He sauntered over and leaned against the open window as if he didn't have a care in the world. "Where you ladies going?" he asked.

Ugh. Days had passed and she still got the creeps from him. "Nursery. I'm going to do some landscaping."

"Making your new home all pretty, huh?" he asked with a tight smile.

Emory looked over at Luna, who was glaring at Brian. "What do you want?" Luna asked him.

Brian barely spared her a glance before he was back to staring down at Emory. "I hear you're originally from the Remsen Pride."

If it was possible to live with a stopped heart, she'd have sworn it no longer beat in her chest. When the trembles started low in her belly, her heart kicked back into gear and went straight into overdrive. "Who told you that?" she barely got past her closing throat.

She was going to pass out. Her breath was coming in short pants and her heart was beating too fast.

"Everyone in the Pride knows it. Turns out, you have a thing for lions."

Without a second thought, Emory threw her car in reverse and literally peeled out of the driveway, not even caring that she probably left black skid marks on Eli's pristine driveway. She hoped she'd run over Brian's foot, too.

How the hell did everyone know about that? Had Eli actually told her secret?

"What did he mean, Em?" Luna asked.

Emory glanced at her, and she had a mixture of worry, fear, and anger etched in the lines of her face and in her glowing gold eyes.

"I can't," she said as she sucked in air. She was hyperventilating. Shit. She needed…what did she need?

She needed her Pack. But she couldn't go there. She couldn't do that to Luna and she didn't want them to see her like this. They'd freak out and think something happened to her and rush out to kill someone. No. She needed to calm herself down and then talk to Eli tonight. How dare he tell anyone about Jace.

Wait…

"Did you know that?"

"About your home Pride being Remsen? How would I know that? You're a wolf, not a lion."

"Eli didn't tell you…about any of it?"

Luna shook her head. If he hadn't told his only sister, why would he tell anyone else? It didn't make sense. It was obvious he didn't trust most of the guys in his Pride and he sure as hell didn't seem too hip on Brian. He'd be the last person her mate would confide in. About *anything*. Let alone his mate's history with another male.

She needed to talk to Eli. She'd have to wait until he got off work, though. He might be Alpha, but he still had a job to do. Brian hadn't threatened her or done anything other than mention Remsen. She had to get that shit out of her head and go on with her day and just pretend that asshole didn't exist.

"Em, why were you with Remsen?" Luna pressed.

"I really don't want to talk it about right now. I'm trying to avoid a full-blown panic attack while I'm driving," she said with a shaky smile.

"You want me to drive?" she offered.

"No. I'm fine. I need the distraction."

Emory wasn't fine. She was freaking out. But she wasn't lying about needing to drive to give herself something to focus on instead of giving in to the panic clawing its way through her system. She had to get herself under control, buy the damn plants like she wanted, and get back to the house. She didn't want Brian or any of the other guys to see any form of weakness from her. She was the Alpha's mate and she'd act like it, damn it.

By the time they got to the local nursery, her heart had slowed down and she was no longer sweating like a pig. That would change the second they stepped from the car into the stifling heat of the green house, but at least it wouldn't be from her nerves.

Luna helped her pick out some pretty bushes and flowers and they loaded them into the backseat of her car and headed back home. If she encountered Brian, she'd just tell him to fuck off and mind his own business. Just practicing the words in her head gave her a little boost of confidence. Who the hell did he think he was, bringing that shit up and obviously lying to her? He might have eavesdropped somehow and learned about her past, but there was no way Eli would tell anyone but his sister about her and Jace.

There were a few people outside their homes, but for the most part, the two streets were empty as she guided the car to Eli's house. Her house. *Their* house. Even as she tried to correct herself, it still didn't feel right. He might live there, but it didn't feel like his home. This might be his Pride, but they didn't feel like his family, not all of them.

It had that same forced feeling that Remsen and Blue Ridge had when she was so young. It was where he lived, they were the people he was supposed to lead, but they weren't his family. Or even friends. They were uneasy acquaintances at best.

Emory backed her car into the driveway so the unloading would be easier. Once they had everything set out to where they'd plant them, she headed to the garage.

Seriously? She'd never seen a more pristine garage in her life. "Where the hell are all your gardening tools? And if you tell me there aren't any after we just left the nursery, I'm not going to be happy." she asked Luna with her hands on her hips.

"Back yard in the shed," Luna said, pointing as she walked around the side of the house.

They gathered everything they'd need and piled them into a wheelbarrow to make it easier to get everything up front at once. No reason to make several trips when she knew she'd be exhausted by the time they were done.

"Why did you get so much?" Luna asked, standing and staring at everything strewn everywhere.

"Oh, please. I don't remember hearing you complain. In fact, pretty sure you picked a lot of this out." Emory winked at Luna and grabbed a shovel to break up the ground under the picture window. It was a blank canvas just begging for some personal touches.

Once she was done with the place, it would look more like a regular suburban home and less like a place from that Stepford Wives movie. Maybe she'd talk Eli into changing the color of the shutters, too. Anything to make the house homier. It might not change how she felt about the Pride but it would help how she felt staying there.

As the hours passed, the sun crossed the sky and began to dip behind the trees. It had to be after seven by now, but still no Eli. He must've gotten stuck at work. And she'd left her phone in her purse in her car. She was too covered in mud, worm poop, and pollen to even attempt to dig through that big thing to check her texts. Besides, if it was important, he'd have called or texted Luna by now.

"Any idea what time it is?" Emory asked Luna as she covered the last flower.

"Time for bed," Luna said, standing and pulling her arms over her head. "I can't remember the last time I worked this hard."

Emory straightened, cracking her back as she leaned and turned toward her kind of sister-in-law. "You've never had a job?"

Luna pursed her lips and cocked one blonde brow. "What do you think?"

"Right. You guys weren't allowed to."

Even though Callie was away from the Pride and had her own life now, she still hadn't gotten a job. Micah was fine with that, but Emory knew Callie was getting bored and restless having nothing to do except hang out with Nova and Rieka all day when everyone was at work.

"Well, you can now. Ever think about what you'd want to do?" Emory asked as she started tossing gardening tools toward the wheelbarrow.

Luna shrugged. "I like kids. And animals. But I don't think I'd be able to work with dogs or anything like that. They tend to freak out whenever I'm nearby."

Right. The whole predator living inside thing would probably send a dog into a panic.

"What about working at a daycare or getting your teaching degree?"

Luna stopped, a spade in her hand. "I'd have to go to school for that. It's too late."

"How old are you?" Emory asked.

"Twenty-three."

Emory snorted. "It's not too late at all. Haven't you ever heard those stories of women going back for their doctorates at, like, eighty?"

"I don't know. People will stare at me." She looked at the tool in her hand and shrugged. "I hate that."

Emory wanted to tell her she was crazy, that no one would even notice the scars, but didn't want to lie to her. There would be people who would stare. There would be people who would ask her where they were from. It was something she had to learn to accept about herself before she could expect anyone else to accept. Emory thought Luna was beautiful, and she was learning it was both inside and out. She just had to see that herself.

"Just think about it. You have a whole world open to you now. You can go to school, get a job, get your own car, whatever you want."

Luna's head was still down, yet Emory saw the wistful smile on her lips. It showed she'd heard Emory. That smile meant she was actually thinking about all the possibilities she now had for her life.

"Dude, I'm beat," Emory said, changing the subject.

"I have blisters," Luna said, studying her palm.

"Eh. They'll become callouses and add character."

"Ew. I don't want callouses," Luna said, wrinkling her nose.

Emory chuckled and tossed the remaining tools into the wheelbarrow and pushed it around the side of the house as Luna cleaned up all the empty containers the flowers had come in. She had to admit, the house looked amazing. She definitely deserved a pat on the back and couldn't wait for Eli to get home to see it. She'd make Luke come outside and admire her work as soon as everything was cleaned up and perfect.

Everything would spread and bloom and fill in the empty spots by mid-summer and she couldn't wait. She should've gotten more marigolds. She loved the pop of yellows and oranges, not to mention they were awesome for deterring pests.

Movement in the shadows caught her eye. She turned her head and squinted. It wasn't fully dark yet, but the house and trees made everything seem darker back there. Turning to look over her shoulder, she was tempted to call Luna down with her. She was creeping herself out.

When she looked back, there was nothing there. It was probably a branch swaying in the breeze or a rabbit skittering away from her. Scanning the area once more, she turned her back and began unloading everything, putting them where she'd found them.

Footsteps slowly made their way through the grass. "Hey. Help me push this in," she called out to Luna as she tried to lift the back tires over the lip of the shed.

A hand reached around her and Emory pulled back quickly. The hand was way too large and masculine to be Luna's. And there stood Brian, a wide grin on his face.

"Didn't mean to scare you," he said, shoving the wheelbarrow in with ease. When he stepped back, he shoved his hands in his pockets.

Okay. He wasn't so creepy standing like that. But she was still ready to tell him to fuck off if he brought up Remsen again.

As he opened his mouth, a cocky smirk on his face, she realized she'd get that chance sooner rather than later.

"You don't remember me," Brian said.

Emory narrowed her eyes as she tilted her head up to really get a look at him. He seemed vaguely familiar, but only because she'd seen him when she'd arrived in Tammen. As far as she knew, he could've been at Big River when they'd attacked her Pack. He could even be one of the loyal Rhett followers.

Regardless, she didn't like him in her personal space, and she really didn't like the way he was watching her, the way his eyes roamed her body and flared gold.

"Am I supposed to?" she asked, stepping to the side to go around him. All she'd have to do was scream and Luke would be there. But she still didn't like being out of sight of everyone else.

"I guess that's fair. You were pretty young when you broke my boy's heart, and his nose, before taking off."

And there went her heart, stopping for a second before kicking into high speed.

"Who are you?"

"I told you. Brian."

"Yeah. You told me your name. How do you know me?"

He shook his head and a disappointed look came over his face. "Guess I didn't make a big enough impression on you back then. Jace and I were best friends before I was shipped off to Tammen."

The world seemed to blur around Brian as his words sank in. Everyone in Tammen didn't know about her past, only Brian. And it was because he'd been there. He'd known her back then. That had been so long ago and he'd obviously grown into a man, yet she still only barely recognized him. That time had been such a nightmare she'd more or less blocked out faces. Every time her mind decided to torture her and take her back to that time, everyone but Jace was just a faceless monster, trying to hold her down, starving her, beating her until she could barely stand.

"You were there?" she asked, struggling to keep her tone steady. She searched in her peripheral for an escape route. She could turn and run the opposite direction, but that would put him at her back. She could Shift, but a male lion would overpower her tiny wolf in a second.

So, she opened her mouth to yell for Luke.

The second her mouth flew wide, Brian's hand slapped over it and he backed her into the shed, her head hitting the wall with enough force to rattle her brains.

Throwing both hands out, she made contact with his face and raked her claws down his cheek. He yanked back, touched his fingertips to the ruined skin, and glared at the blood.

"Are you serious? After everything I've done for you?"

Her eyes widened and she kicked out. She searched deep for her wolf, begged her to help. And, apparently, he could tell she was trying to Shift.

Drawing his hand into a fist, he let it fly directly at her face. She managed to duck to the side, but he still got her right in the temple.

Oh god. Where the hell was Luna? Why wasn't she looking for Emory yet?

Her vision blurred with his last hit, and she was having a hard time keeping her eyes open. She had to stay alert. By the way he was struggling with his belt, she knew the second she fell unconscious, this fucker would have his way with her body.

Not. Fucking. Happening.

If she didn't let them assault her as a young, skinny kid, she sure as fuck wouldn't let that happen now.

Emory swung as hard as she could, even though her strength was fading quickly, and kicked at Brian's shins and tried to knee him in the crotch. She'd crush his balls before she let him near her.

"Fuck. Would you calm the hell down? I'm trying to help you?"

She shook her head and tried to bite his hand. Trying to help her? Was he fucking crazy? How was raping a woman helping?

"You don't belong here and you know it. Everyone knows you hate these people. Once you're carrying a Remsen cub, you can go back home. Even with Jace dead, I'm sure the Alpha will take you back."

What. The. Fuck.

Jace was dead. And this asshole was going to rape her, try to get her pregnant with his cub so she could go back to Remsen? Did he miss the part where she ran away? She left there on purpose because they were trying to do exactly what he was attempting.

Screaming into his hand, she continued to fight, even after he struck her again. Shit. Her legs were going to give out. She could barely hold her damn head up.

Brian's body lurched against hers and she peeled her lids back to see Luna on his back, her mouth wide as she screamed and scratched at his eyes.

He couldn't fight Luna off and contain Emory. The second his hold on her released, she crumpled to the ground and crawled toward a shovel, yielding it in front of her like a bat. But she had zero strength left and couldn't get it to swing hard enough to do any damage. Didn't mean she wouldn't keep trying.

A bellow rattled her ear drums and she dropped the shovel to clap her hands over her ears. Her head hurt. Her face hurt. Everything hurt.

Brian's body was wrenched back and out of her view. And then the two lionesses she'd been staying with were there, trying to help Luna pull Emory off the ground. She tried to get her feet under her, but her legs kept buckling beneath her, bringing her to her knees.

"Kill him," she whispered to Luke. She knew he probably couldn't hear her. It didn't matter. She knew Brian would no longer be a threat to her once the Blackwater bear was done with him.

Chapter Eleven

Eli held the phone to his ear, trying to make sense of the screaming on the other line.

"Luna. Calm down. I can't understand a word you're saying."

"Get home now!" she screamed and the call ended.

Oh god. Emory.

Throwing the wrench he'd been using to the ground, he sprinted for his car and fishtailed out of the parking lot. He barely checked for traffic as he pulled onto the highway to the sounds of a honking horn and tears screeching as someone slammed on their brakes.

Something had happened to Emory or else she would've been the one to call. He ran every scenario through his head, tried to think of anyone who'd want to hurt her. She hadn't shown any fear lately.

Except over Brian.

Eli knew nothing about Brian except he'd been one of the kids who'd joined him in Tammen when they were sent away to train as enforcers.

Remsen. As in the Pride she'd escaped.

He was a fucking idiot. Why hadn't he put two and two together? Then again, Brian would've been gone before Emory had arrived, just like Eli had been. There should be no connection there.

No. He was looking at worse case scenarios. She was gardening today; maybe she'd cut herself or gotten hurt somehow. Luna tended to panic. Emory must be bleeding and it freaked his sister out.

Please, God. Let that be all.

He got home within six minutes of hanging up with Luna. There were two trucks parked in his yard. They hadn't even pulled into his driveway; just drove right up to his front door. This couldn't be some cut hand if her Pack was already there.

Eli threw his door open and ran for the door. Every step he felt like he was running through tar, like he was in one of those weird dreams where he couldn't get his legs to work right. He had to get to Emory.

There were people all over his yard, their attention toward the side or back. Pushing through the crowd, his heart thundered until all he could hear was the blood whooshing in his ears and his own breath sawing through his lungs.

He pushed forward until he was staring down at his severely battered mate. Her face was swollen and purple bruises had already formed. They'd be gone by morning, but the cut on her right cheek and above her top lip would leave a scar.

"What the fuck happened?" he said, his lion's growl wrapping around every syllable.

His legs gave out the second he was near Emory and he dropped to his knees heavily. Holy shit. There was dried blood in her hair and, by the crimson rag in Luna's hand, there had been a lot more.

"Brian," Luna said, barely glancing up at him before going back to staring at Emory.

Tears welled in her eyes, and Eli searched the faces crowded around as everything took on a deep red hue. "Where the fuck is he?" he growled out.

"Brother, calm down," Gray said, setting a hand on his shoulder. "You won't help her if you Shift right now." Her entire Pack was there, even Callie who'd only been gone from Tammen for a few months.

"Where. Is. That motherfucker?" he said again, lifting his eyes to Gray.

Bodies parted. Luke and Colton were standing over Brian in their bear forms as Brian swayed on his knees. He'd definitely taken a beating, but the mother fucker was still alive. He was still breathing after touching his mate.

Not just touching her; he'd assaulted her, left permanent scars on her.

"What happened?" Eli growled out as he glared at Brian.

"I heard him. I didn't get there in time, but I heard him talking. He was going to get her pregnant and take her back to Remsen," Luna said, her voice thick with emotion. "I'm so sorry. I should've gotten there sooner."

Eli's eyes darted to Luke. No. The bear was the one who was supposed to be protecting Emory. And he'd failed Eli's mate. Once Brian was out of the picture, Eli planned on letting Luke now exactly how pissed he was at his failure.

Stalking toward Brian, he halted only a second when a soft hand landed on his arm. "They've got him. You need to be with Emory," Callie's sweet voice said.

Eli glanced over his shoulder at Emory. She was begging him with her eyes, begging him to be with her, to hold her as she huddled on the ground, Nova and Luna on either side, their arms wrapped around her shoulders.

"She's supposed to be with Remsen. The whore attacked her mate and ran off to slum with the wolves."

Brian's words stopped Eli from turning and going to Emory.

"What the fuck did you just say?" he asked, lowering his head and cringing as his fangs dropped from his gums as his lion forced its way out.

"She's a fucking Remsen breeder. She belongs with our family Pride, asshole. You know that. You can't mate a claimed female."

Their family Pride. Eli might have been born into Remsen, but they weren't his family. He refused to be connected to anyone who'd throw their daughters away, who'd sell their own children off.

And this son of a bitch sure as fuck wasn't his family.

"You tried to…" His jaw was cracking and he couldn't form any more words. His lion was coming and there wasn't a thing he could do to stop it.

****

Emory couldn't stop shaking. Fear and anger warred inside of her. How did that happen? Her guys were supposed to be keeping an eye on things, yet Brian was able to catch her off-guard. What would've happened had Luna not come running at him, screaming like a banshee? He'd beat the fight out of Emory, so she wasn't even sure if she could've kept him from…

She squeezed her eyes shut as Eli stalked toward Brian. Luke and Colton stayed still, their eyes on him as his entire body began to vibrate. It was like he was a one-man earthquake. And then Brian opened his mouth and spewed some of the most disgusting words she'd ever heard pieced together.

"You tried to…" Every word was a guttural growl and then Eli the man was gone. In his place stood an enormous lion, his mane blowing in the constant breeze. He was magnificent. He was also terrifying.

He lifted his head and released a bone jarring roar and charged Brian. People were yelling, running for him, trying to stop him.

Yet Emory could do nothing more than watch as his mouth clamped around Brian's throat and shook him violently. Brian didn't even have time to Shift before Eli attacked him. He was dead within seconds, hanging limp from Eli's jaws.

And Eli still didn't Shift back. He dragged Brian's body up the hill and around the corner, out of Emory's sight. Good. She was glad he was dead. But it had been too quick and painless for what he'd done to her and what he'd tried to do.

"Take me home," she said, her voice raspy from her screams and the pressure Brian had put on her throat.

She wobbled to her feet with the help of Nova and Luna, but Tristan was there, scooping her into his arms with one arm behind her back and the other under her knees. She wrapped her arms around his neck and buried her face in his neck as he carried her up the hill and to his truck.

Pulling away, she snorted at how her Pack had parked when they'd rushed there. There would be major divets in the yard when they all left. At least they hadn't ruined the pretty garden she was leaving behind.

Tears welled in her eyes as she stared at the house she'd attempted to make home, even if she knew it wasn't permanent. She and Eli hadn't even been able to make love again in the time she'd been there, but they'd grown closer. She'd learned his sounds when he slept, his routine every morning. And now she was leaving.

As Tristan set her gently in the front seat of his truck, Reed climbed into the back. He laid a hand on her shoulder and squeezed gently.

"I should've been here," he said, his voice thick.

"No. It would've happened someday, regardless of who was there."

Luke had been the one to stay with her that day and he'd had no idea anything was happening. Unless someone glued themselves to her side twenty-four/seven, there was no way to ever truly keep her safe from people like Brian. There would always be people out there who thought women were nothing more than property, even with the laws changing.

She had fangs and claws and still wasn't able to protect herself. She'd worked so hard to find her inner strength and had tried to get Luna and the other women to be strong, to see the world as a safer place. Yet, here she was with bruises and cuts on her face from a member of her mate's Pride.

She'd tried to see these people as hers, but it was almost impossible now. Even though a few had come running and helped Luke beat the piss out of Brian. Even after her two other roommates had helped Luna drag Emory away from the shed and cleaned her up before anyone got there.

They weren't her people. Big River was her family and that was who she needed to be with, maybe forever.

As Tristan pulled the truck away, Emory turned her eyes away from Luna's sad face. Tears tracked down her cheeks as she watched Emory leave Tammen. And then they rose to where her brother was standing over Brian's dead body, growling and hissing at anyone who came near.

Eli's eyes raised to hers as she passed and watched her with an unexplainable look on his face. It was as if his lion didn't recognize her, as if all humanity in Eli's body was gone.

He lifted his head and roared again as she passed him and Emory slapped her hands over her ears. That sound was full of heartache and she couldn't stand to hear it, not with her own pain in her heart.

She hated to leave him behind. She hated that she was hurting him. And she hated Brian for putting them in this position. She'd just call him later. Maybe they could pick back up the dating thing and meet in the woods a few times a week.

Smiling sadly, she leaned her head against the seat and watched as the gate to Tammen territory passed her by. She needed to be home. She needed her house. She needed her family to heal.

****

Her Pack fussed over her the second she'd climbed from the truck. Tristan tried to carry her into her house, but she pushed his hands away and trudged the distance. Her body ached, but not nearly as bad as her heart.

She already missed her mate. It felt like a part of her own soul had been ripped away from her. It had barely been twenty minutes and her wolf was already whining and begging for her mate.

Standing in the middle of her living room, she looked around at the tiny space. She'd missed her home. She'd missed sleeping in her bed. Or any bed for that matter. Yet, even though this was her space and had been for years, it felt hollow, empty, and lacking.

Because her mate wasn't there. Eli wasn't there to fill the space with his energy and his big body. The closest she'd ever get to cohabitating with him was the nine days she'd spent on his couch with one of her friends crashing on the floor just feet away.

Shit. She'd left her belongings back there. Her toothbrush, hair brush, and a lot of her clothes were still sitting on a bag on Eli's floor. And she didn't have it in her to return there or even go into public to get new ones.

Feet clomped up her stairs but no one knocked. After glancing through the window, she smiled as she shook her head. Tristan had positioned himself on the front porch, and by the thick book in his hand, it looked like he didn't plan to leave anytime soon.

Before heading out there, she showered, hissing from the pain when the hot water hit a gash on her scalp she wasn't even aware was there. That bastard had done as much damage as possible, just trying to shut her up and make her more compliant.

And now he was dead. And her mate had gone a little feral. And she was crying in the shower alone.

Emory leaned her head against the cool tile of her little corner shower and let the tears flow. She let the anger pulse through her. She let the fear make itself known. And then she stood up straight, squared her shoulders, dried off, and stomped across the room to sit with her Pack.

It would take time to get over this, she knew that. She also knew she'd need their support to heal.

"Hey," she said as she lowered beside Tristan.

He nudged her with his shoulder, but didn't raise his eyes from his book. Taking a closer look, she chuckled. "Is that Nova's new book?"

"Yep," he said, turning the book so Emory could see the cover.

"Guess you're done pretending you've never read her stuff."

"About us," he said with a shrug.

And then they sat in silence. Which was fine with her. She'd always been at ease just being around Tristan. She didn't need him to talk or tell her everything would be alright. She knew that. She'd been through worse and had come out stronger. No. He just told her he was there for her by literally being there. His presence was the best comfort he could offer.

"You okay?" Nova asked from her front porch. Her dad, Alan, was standing there with her, Rieka in his arms, as they both watched her expectantly.

"Not yet," Emory admitted.

Nova nodded in understanding while her dad stared at her with bright blue wolf eyes. He'd had to stay behind to watch after the baby while her Pack rushed to her side. This was the first time he'd gotten a good look at her face and the rage showed in the deep furrow between his brows.

"Can I do anything?" Alan asked, handing Rieka over to Nova and climbing down her stairs to stand in front of Emory.

"I'd ask you to kill someone, but that's already been done."

As Gray, Nova and Rieka, Callie and Micah, and Reed all came to stand in a semi-circle around her, the tears broke free again. She dropped her face into her hands and let them fall while several hands laid on her shoulder, the top of her head, and made slow circles on her back.

She was home with her people, but her heart was still back in Tammen.

Chapter Twelve

Emory lied in bed with Tristan asleep on the floor. When she couldn't get him to leave her front porch, she'd invited him in. They'd talked, she'd cried, she'd drank a lot of wine Nova had bought her, and then she'd passed out.

Something had woken her up, but there was nothing out of the ordinary other than a snoring man in her house. She'd know that snore anywhere after hearing it for so many years.

No. It was something outside.

There it was again. It was a deep chuffing sound, bordering between a growl and a bark.

Pushing the blanket away, she tiptoed to the door in time to hear it again, but it sounded like it was coming from deep in the woods. She didn't know what that was, but something about it called to her.

With a quick glance back at Tristan, she pulled the door open and peeked outside. She wanted to investigate, but she'd never been one of those women from the movies who wandered out on their own in the middle of the night after going through something so traumatic.

"Tristan," she whispered, trying to wake him up without scaring him.

She looked back out the door then back to Tristan. "Hey, Tristan. Wake up."

He stirred, groaned, then shot straight up, his eyes wide.

"That's so creepy when you do that?"

"What's wrong?" he said, climbing to his feet still half-asleep.

"Do you—"

There was the sound again.

Tristan looked toward the door, to Emory, then crossed the room and yanked her inside. He stepped outside. "Gray's here," he said, jerking his head toward the front yard.

Emory stepped out behind Tristan, his arm out so she couldn't go any further, and stared wide-eyed at Gray and Micah.

"It's Eli," Gray said, dragging a hand down his face. "He's been out here for hours."

Had he been making that sound the whole time and she'd just heard it?

Shuffling off her porch, she took a few steps in the direction of the woods. Was he in their territory? It sounded too far away.

"He's at our spot," she whispered as she realized why he sounded so far away.

He'd gone to the place where they'd made love. He'd wanted to check on his mate, yet showed enough respect to Gray to keep his distance, so he'd gone to the place where they'd truly connected.

"Em," Reed called out as she began to jog in that direction.

She slowed and looked over her shoulder. "He's in our spot. He's calling me."

"Fuck," Reed said, waving her on as he ran to catch up with her. "Don't look at me like that. You're not going anywhere without one of us for the next ten years," he said as he jogged alongside her.

She didn't need a bodyguard. She knew it was Eli. She'd know his sound even if she'd never heard it before. Her wolf knew him. Her wolf knew his scent, knew all about his animal.

Several sets of feet were crunching in the dry grass and leaves behind her as she ran to her mate. Tristan and Micah were following behind, ensuring her safety.

Heavy steps were running toward her now as if Eli had heard her coming.

The second his dark mane came into view, Eli hunched into himself and Shifted into his human body. He was running again, stark naked, the moon casting silver across his body, but he didn't seem to notice that he was on full display for the guys in her Pack.

They didn't slow, just like the first time they'd met there, just crashed into each other's arms.

Eli's lips were everywhere, her forehead, her cheeks, her nose, and finally her lips. "I'm so sorry," he breathed against her skin between each kiss. "I'm so sorry. I should've been there." Another kiss. "I'm so sorry."

And she was crying again. This time with relief. She was still scared. She was still pissed. But in Eli's arms, she felt whole.

Someone cleared their throat from behind her and pulled them out of their moment.

"Come back," Tristan said with a jerk of his head.

"Not yet. I need my mate," Emory said through tears.

"Both," Tristan said, turned and walked back through the woods.

Micah and Reed waited with crossed arms as she looked up at Eli. He nodded, scooped her in his arms, and carried her out of the woods. She hadn't even noticed she was barefoot, hadn't paid any attention to the twigs and pine cones digging into the soles of her feet. All she knew was Eli. She had to get to Eli.

Gray, Nova, and Callie were waiting just outside Gray's house when they cleared the tree line. There was curiosity and something else in their eyes. Relief? Happiness? Wariness? She couldn't tell. All she knew was how she felt at that moment.

Like her heart had come home.

Eli set Emory on her feet gently, his arm instantly going around her shoulders as he bent to press a kiss to her temple.

"I still can't let you live in our territory, but you're welcome to be with Emory here. I don't want her back in your Pride," Gray said with a nod.

"I'm not going back there," Emory whispered, dropping her head. "I'm sorry, Eli. I can't."

He squeezed her to his side and wrapped his other arm around her, holding her to his chest tightly. "You never have to step a fucking foot there again."

"Dude, couldn't you have at least brought some pants?"

Nova giggled and ran back to her house. When she came back, she was carrying a pair of Gray's sweats. "These might be a little short, but they should fit your waist and cover your weenie."

"You never cease to shock me," Reed said, covering his eyes with his hand.

Eli pulled away just long enough to pull the pants over his butt, then he was back to holding Emory tightly again. He was so warm and smelled like forest, fur, and something unique to him. It was an earthy, spicy scent that she wanted to rub all over her so she could smell him all day every day.

Nova shrugged with a smirk. It felt so good to be around them. They were odd and funny and it felt normal. It felt perfect, especially with Eli right there in the middle of it all.

Gray led the group to the lawn chairs and sat beside his mate. He glanced up at the house, as if checking for any sounds from his baby, before turning back to Eli.

"What happened when we left?"

Eli pushed a hand through his hair and shifted his weight in the chair. He was ashamed. Whether it was because he hadn't been there to protect Emory, because it had been a member of both his family and current Pride who'd attacked her, or the total loss of control over his animal, Emory wasn't sure.

"He's been buried."

"Should've just left the fucker out for the crows," Micah said, gripping Callie's hand tightly. His eyes had that constant blue glow as he stared at Eli.

Eli huffed out a humorless laugh. "I thought about it." His eyes found Emory's again. "I'm so fucking sorry."

"It wasn't your fault, Eli," Emory said, leaning into his touch when he cupped her cheek.

"How many others are like him there?" Micah asked.

Eli shook his head. "If you'd asked me that a day ago, I would've said none. I thought I ran those fuckers off. But now? I won't lie. I don't know."

"What about the other women?" Callie asked. "Now that Emory's gone, what's going to happen to them?"

"Same thing that happened before I got there. They'll keep themselves locked behind closed doors and pray to get through another day." Emory leaned onto Eli's shoulder and thought about Luna and Petra and Amber and even Fancy Pants. They didn't deserve that life. They deserved to find happiness and to feel safe.

And that would never happen as long as they stayed within that Pride.

"There's got to be a way to get them out," Callie said, mimicking Emory's thoughts.

They didn't have room in Big River for all the lionesses. Maybe she could ask their friends to each give up one room to fit a few of them. But that still wouldn't be enough.

"Shame they can't just start their own Pride," Nova said with a snort.

Shame they couldn't...or could they?

"Has anyone checked out that land back there?" Emory said, jerking her chin toward the property just behind theirs.

"You mean Booty Call Land?" Reed said, then shook his head when Gray frowned at him in confusion. Apparently, no one had filled him in on Emory and Eli's midnight loving a few weeks back.

"Yeah, that," Emory said as she tried to hide her embarrassed giggle.

"What about it?" Gray asked.

Eli was staring down at her with wide eyes and a wider smile. "Anyone have their phone?" he asked, looking around.

Callie held hers up and tossed it to Eli. He caught it and started tapping on the screen until he turned it around to show Emory the sale page and information.

"Well, shit. Might as well be a million dollars," Emory said when she saw the price. "There's no way we can come up with that and there's no way we can get a loan."

"I can," Nova said, holding her hand up and sitting straight up in her chair. "I have impeccable credit."

"And you've already been in enough trouble for being too public," Gray said with a smile and a shake of his head.

Emory loved to watch the two of them, loved to watch the way Gray tried so damn hard to pretend he was mad or even shocked by his mate. But it was obvious he loved every little thing about her, even when she was being outrageous. Like suggesting she get a loan for ten acres for a group of lionesses she'd never met.

The next hour was filled with easy conversation and, for a while, Emory felt like herself. The fear and anger had taken a backseat and she as able to enjoy having Eli with her family. He looked like he'd always been there, like he belonged there.

Gray had said he couldn't live in the territory, but he'd said Eli could stay with Emory. And she planned on making him stay that night. She needed the comfort only his arms could provide. She needed his body heat pressed up against hers. She needed...

She needed her mate.

"I'm gong to bed. Rieka will be up in a couple of hours screaming for my boob," Nova said, stretching her arms over her head as she stood.

"Gross, Nova," Reed complained, standing and heading to his own house.

Everyone left and she was there with Eli. He was staring at her again. "You were really thinking about buying that place for the lionesses," he said.

"Yeah."

She couldn't stop her eyes from drifting to his mouth. His tongue peeked out and she smiled. Guess it wasn't only girls whose lips suddenly got dry with so much attention.

"I am so—"

"Stop," she said, placing her fingertips over his lips. "I don't want to talk about it for the rest of the night. Morning. Whatever. I don't even want to think about it."

He held her hand to his mouth by her wrist and feathered kisses against each finger.

"Okay," he said, standing and pulling her to her feet. Just like he had in the woods, he lifted her into his arms and carried her up her stairs and into her house.

He laid her gently onto the futon and sat on the floor in front of her.

"What are you doing?"

"You need some sleep," he said.

"Uh, you're sleeping beside me. This is the first time we won't be cramped on the couch. Get your ass up here."

He chuckled deep and lifted to sit directly beside her, pulling her against him as he laid back. But he didn't do anything else. Didn't try to take off her clothes or make out with her. Just held her, his heart *thump thump thumping* against her ear.

"You're scared to touch me," she whispered into the dark.

"I don't want to hurt you."

"You won't."

Eli pulled away so he could look into her eyes. "When that beautiful face is healed and your mind no longer returns to that shed and…I won't even say his name, then I'll make love to you. I can wait."

"I can't," she said, poking out her bottom lip.

Eli chuckled again and kissed the tip of her nose. Instead of taking her cue and rolling on top of her, he just pulled her until she was fully lying on top of him, their bodies lined from chest to…well, not toe because hers hit his shins.

"Get some sleep. I shouldn't have woken you up."

Emory frowned at the wall. "How long have you been out there?" she asked.

His shoulder moved in a slight shrug. "Not sure. I wasn't really conscious until about an hour ago."

According to Gray, he'd been out there for hours, calling to her. Not Eli. His lion. His lion had been crying out for its mate. He'd found the spot Emory loved so much and waited for her.

"Goodnight," she whispered.

Eli kissed the top of her head. "Goodnight, baby."

****

Emory rolled onto her side. She opened her eyes, searching for Eli, yet her bed was empty.

Had she dreamed that last night? Had he not come for her?

The toilet flushed and water ran in her bathroom. She released the breath she hadn't realized she'd been holding.

He had come for her. He'd called out to her and had been more or less welcomed by the Pack. Well, welcomed might be a little strong. Gray agreed to let him sleepover but just to keep Emory happy and away from Tammen.

He really didn't need to worry. There wasn't a chance in hell she'd ever set foot near that place again. She wasn't even sure if she'd be able to leave her land for a while. The last thing she wanted was to run into any lions from the Pride. And she didn't want to have to face any of the bears from Blackwater and hear any I-told-you-so remarks. At least her Pack was keeping that to themselves. For now. She was actually a little surprised Reed wasn't giving her shit about him always being right.

It was only the first day back. It would probably come eventually.

The curtain separating the bathroom from the rest of the house pulled back and Eli was framed by the light from behind. He reached over and flipped off the light and Emory got a good look at his face.

He looked tired.

"Did you get any sleep?" she asked, grabbing her phone from the floor and checking the time. They'd slept until almost noon. Her eyes whipped up to his face. "Did you call your work and let them know you'd be late?"

His brows pulled together slightly. "It's Saturday. I don't work today."

It was already the weekend? She'd gotten so mixed up the past week she hadn't realized what day it was. She'd had to call in yesterday. She'd been taking off so many days lately, it was just a matter of time before her job let her go for being unreliable.

He crossed the room wearing nothing but the pair of sweats he'd borrowed from Gray and Emory took the opportunity to check out his tattoos, stare at his body, just admire every inch of her mate.

Eli sat on the edge of the futon and pushed the hair from Emory's face. "You were serious last night, weren't you?"

She frowned up at him. "About what?"

"About getting that land for the lionesses."

"Well, yeah. We could even live there, too. It would be our own Pride."

His face softened as his eyes skimmed over her face. "Even after what happened you still want to help my people."

She pursed her lips and her brows raised. "Not all of them. Just the women," she admitted. "I'm not a saint. I just want them to have the same kind of life I've had. Someone needs to give them the opportunity. I just wish I made more money."

His brows were pinched in concentration as he toyed with a strand of her hair. "We'll figure something out."

"I'm not going back to Tammen, Eli. I can't."

His head wagged side to side slowly. "No. I'd never ask you to do that. But I still have to be there until we can find somewhere for the lionesses."

"You really care about them, don't you?"

His frown deepened. "Got to be honest, kind of hurts my feelings that you even have to ask that by now."

"That's not what I—"

His smile was forced. "I know what you meant." He bent over and pressed a kiss to her nose. "Gray came by an hour ago."

Emory looked at the door and looked back at him with wide eyes. "How long have you been up?"

He was looking through the front window. "I don't think I actually slept."

That explained the dark circles under his eyes. "You just laid here listening to me snore?"

He snorted. "You don't snore. And yeah. I just wanted to hold you. I couldn't make myself get out of your bed."

Eli stretched out beside her and pulled her against his chest like he had last night until she was lying on top of him. Pushing it, she sat up and threw either leg across his hips until she was straddling him. He was so hard and ready, pressed against her core. Grinding against him, they both moaned when the only thing separating them were two thin pieces of cotton, her panties and his sweats.

"We could always go for a quickie," Emory said.

"No you can't. We're all sitting out here waiting for you," Reed called through the walls. "And I really don't feel like listening to you bang."

Her cheeks heated as she dropped over Eli and buried her face in his chest with a groan. "No privacy," she said, her voice muffled against his skin.

His deep chuckle rumbled against her as his hands smoothed up and down her back. "We've got the rest of our lives."

Those words hit her right in the chest. She hadn't really considered the fact she had a mate for the rest of her life. She'd been so focused on the present, on getting to know each other, on trying to make everyone happy and make sure everyone around her was safe. He was right, though. They had the next sixty years to learn everything about each other, and that included what made the other person moan the loudest.

Lifting back up, she sat on top of him and stared down at him. She had words trapped inside of her for a while and she couldn't hold them in any longer.

"I got your text," she blurted out. His confused frown made her giggle softly. "You told me you loved me."

"Sending that scared the shit out of me," he admitted.

"I love you, too," she said.

He gasped softly and didn't breathe for a few seconds. And then he wrapped his arms around her and pulled her back to his chest and hugged her until she had to wiggle free a little just to get air in her lungs.

"Fuck, Emory. I love you so much. I've loved you since the day I saw you. I've loved you from the day I heard your sexy little voice."

"My voice is not sexy," she said with a smile.

"It's the most beautiful, sexiest sound in the world to me."

"Oh my gawd! Will you guys come on? You're killing me with all this mushy crap," Reed yelled.

"Leave them alone. It's sweet," Callie said with a tinkling laugh.

With a roll of her eyes, Emory climbed off Eli and pulled on some clothes. Whatever her Pack had to say better be important if they were interrupting her moment with her mate. Eli followed her outside to find every single one of them sitting in the lawn chairs, watching her front door expectantly.

"About time," Reed said and turned his back on her. But she hadn't missed the wide smile before he turned.

"Whatever. You're just jealous," Emory said.

"Why does everyone keep saying that?" Reed asked Tristan, who smiled and shrugged. Like he was ever going to get a full answer from Tristan.

Eli wrapped his hand around Emory's and led her to the chairs, waiting until she was sitting before dragging a chair closer and sitting beside her. He immediately grabbed her hand and kept it tightly in his as they waited for the Pack meeting to start.

"You look good," Nova said, leaning closer to inspect Emory's face.

"Thanks?" Emory said, pulling back.

"No. I mean the bruises are all gone."

"Same as you, Nova. I heal quick."

Nova shrugged and reached a hand forward to touch Emory's face.

Emory batted her hand away and pulled away, trying to avoid Nova's fingers. "Stop. What are you doing, weirdo?"

Nova, being who she was, started poking the air around Emory. "What? I'm not touching you."

"You're such a child," Emory said, but she couldn't help the laugh. Damn, she'd missed this. She'd missed sitting around the fire pit with her family and being silly. She'd missed how easy it was to be with them, unlike the connection she'd tried to force on the Tammen Pride.

"Eli said you came over earlier," Emory said to Gray, attempting to ignore Nova as she continued to poke the air.

Nova stopped, smiled widely, and turned to stare at her mate, waiting for his news.

"I'm Alpha, but my mate has overruled me in something," Gray said, his face emotionless.

"Eli can stay here?" Emory asked, sitting up straight and feeling hope bloom in her chest.

"You know he can't, Emory. And it has nothing to do with my orders. He had his own Pride to look after. He can't leave those women to the assholes left behind."

"Then what?" Emory asked. What could Nova have overruled Gray on? Was he originally going to ban Emory as well since she was mated to a lion?

"Okay, listen," Nova said, scooting until she was sitting on the edge of her chair. "You remember my book I wrote about all of us?"

Emory looked at Tristan. It had been the same book he'd been reading on her porch last night. "Yeah. Country Virgin," Emory answered and snorted at the name, just as she had when Nova had told her the first time what she planned to name the new book.

"That one. So yeah…it's kind of doing really, really good. Like, I'm-officially-rich good."

"That's awesome, Nova. Congrats," Emory said.

"That's not the news," Nova said, waving off Emory's congratulations. "My next royalty check will cover the down payment on that property back there," she said, pointing toward the tree line.

Emory's heart began to race and her hand tightened around Eli's. "What?"

"Blackwater and Ravenwood have offered up some money to buy it outright. Between our Pack and their Clan and Pride, we can buy it free and clear," Nova said, her smile so wide Emory was surprised it didn't reach her ears.

"You guys are going to buy us property?" Emory whispered.

"Not just you. The women of Tammen. And any woman trying to leave a Pride or whatever," Gray said. "You guys can make it some kind of refuge or some shit. Make it a safe haven. The women can build their own homes like Callie had done, find jobs, and have real lives," Gray said.

Tears blurred Emory's vision as she looked to each of her family members. They each smiled and nodded. Holy shit. This was happening.

"I'm going to help get them comfortable. Like, when you guys take them shopping, I'm going to go so you don't overwhelm them like you did with me," Callie said.

"We overwhelmed you?" Nova asked.

Micah snorted. "You overwhelm everyone," he said with a straight face, but Emory saw the slight uptick of his lips.

"Is this for real?" Emory said, her throat tight as she tried to keep the emotion out of her voice.

"Well, it's either that or I'll just end up blowing my money on more trinkets," Nova said, leaning back in her seat, that smile still wide on her face.

"You have got to stop breaking into people's houses," Micah said, crossing his arms over his chest.

"Callie doesn't mind," Nova said.

Emory tuned out her Pack and turned to stare up into Eli's face. His mouth was hanging open and his eyes were wide as he realized they weren't playing. Her Pack and her friends were going to help them get some land so they could be together and help the lionesses. Not just the lionesses from Tammen, but any female who needed help.

"I have a stipulation, though," Gray said, raising his voice to be heard over his bickering Pack.

"And that is?" Emory said. She didn't even care what he said. He could tell her they had to name the Pride after him and she'd agree to it at that point.

"No males who've ever owned a female."

Eli nodded hard once as if he'd already thought of that.

"I'm not going to say no males, because the females might want to find their true mates at some point. But I don't want any of those assholes who claimed women against their will anywhere near my mate or my Pack."

"Agreed," Eli said.

She knew he'd been kicking males out as they fought against the new rules, but this was taking it one step further. And she was fully on board with Gray's edict.

Emory smiled up at Eli, tears glistening in her eyes. As one rolled down her cheek, he brushed it away with his fingertips and leaned down to press his lips to hers. He held there, breathing her in until someone chuckled.

Nova. The perv was watching them with a wistful smile on her lips.

"I know you don't want pups," Nova said, making Emory pull away from Eli. "But if you get a cat or something, could you name it after me?"

Eli threw his head back and barked out a laugh as Emory leaned against Nova's shoulder and smiled. She'd name every pet, plant, and vegetable after her from here until she was lowered into the ground after what she was doing for Emory and Eli.

Chapter Thirteen

"We are gathered here today to—"

"We know why we're here. Skip that part," Reed said, cutting off Alan off as he read from something he'd printed off the computer.

Emory leaned into Eli's side as they watched Callie and Micah finally get married. Just like Nova, she'd opted for a small wedding on their land. Not Big River land. Hope Pride land, the place Emory's family and friends had bought.

There were only a few tiny houses similar to those in Big River dotting the area, but the insides weren't complete. That didn't stop Luna, Amber, and Petra from moving in the second they were delivered.

There had been so much mud after the last rain, but Emory had just pulled on some cute, daisy covered rain boots and slogged through in her white sundress. She'd also opted to forego the traditional wedding gown for something appropriate for the weather and a lot more comfortable.

Micah stood in a pair of jeans and a collared, short-sleeved white polo type shirt, his gaze glued to his soon-to-be-wife. They were a picture of true and deep love as they listened to Alan read a poem Callie had chosen.

Callie had even chosen a time when the sun would be setting behind them, casting her in the most beautiful glow. The whole thing was so romantic and made Emory think of all the possibilities for her future with Eli.

"I, Callie Marie Taylor, take you Micah, to be my mate for as long as there is breath in my lungs and my heart is beating."

Nova sighed loudly and made a few people chuckle.

"I, Micah Anthony Mathews, take you Callie, to be my mate for as long as there is breath in my lungs and my heart is beating."

Eli's arm tightened around Emory's shoulders as Alan stepped back while Micah and Callie embraced. When their kiss deepened, a few guys from the crowd whistled and yelled while the girls giggled softly.

Luna, Petra, and Amber sat silently beside Emory, their smile sweet as they watched what life with their real mate could be. Emory couldn't help but feel for them, even if they finally seemed happy. All the time they'd spent with their mates, they'd never experienced the kind of love on display at this makeshift wedding.

But they would. Someday. Emory was determined to help them find their mate, whether they liked it or not. If she had to play Cupid, she would sharpen up her arrows and start looking.

As the ceremony came to a close, everyone began to rise and situate the chairs so it was easier for everyone to talk. Nova had bought a bunch of tables to hold the food, and the bear Clan and panther Pride had volunteered to provide the food.

Everything was perfect. All her favorite people in the world were there. Even if Luke was careful to avoid even looking in Emory's direction. She knew he blamed himself for what happened, but it wasn't his fault. Brian had watched for an opportunity; one way or another, he would've come for her.

Someday, she just hoped Luke would forgive himself, because she'd forgiven him months ago. Even the scars on her face were faded to almost nothing and had become a conversation starter with humans. She loved to tell them she was attacked by a lion just to watch them laugh and roll their eyes.

Eli tugged her hand and dragged her away from the crowd. "Do you want this someday?" he asked her, nuzzling her neck.

"What?" she breathed out, tilting her head back to give him better access. If he was talking about what he was currently doing, then yeah, she wanted a lot of that. And not someday. Immediately.

"A wedding. Do you want to get married?"

Emory pulled back, her eyes going wide. "Are you asking me to marry you?"

"Not technically," he said with a chuckle. "You looked so happy watching Callie and Micah."

"I was. For them. I don't need that, Eli. I just need you."

"You have me."

"Then I have everything."

She never liked being in the spotlight. And if they had any kind of ceremony, she'd be up there in front of everyone they knew and she'd end up making a fool of herself.

"No. I don't need a wedding. Feel free to write me a poem, though," she said, rising onto her tiptoes to press a kiss to his lips. "And then read it to me in the buff."

Eli threw his head back and laughed. "I love you so much," he said.

She hugged him around the waist, resting her cheek against his chest. "I love you, Eli. Forever. Even without a ceremony."

CHARACTER INDEX

Big River Pack
Grayson (Gray) Harvey – Alpha – wolf
Micah Matthrews– Second – wolf/coyote hybrid
Reed – wolf
Tristan – wolf
Emory Jamison– wolf
Nova Harvey – wolf – mate to Gray
Callie Taylor – mate to Micah

Blackwater Clan
Carter – Alpha – bear
Colton – bear
Luke – bear
Noah – bear – owner of Moe's Tavern

Ravenwood Pride
Aron – Alpha – panther
Mason – panther
Brax – panther – brother to Daxon
Daxon – panther – brother to Brax

Deathport Pack
~~Anson – Alpha – wolf~~
Felix – Second – wolf
Barrett – wolf
Kaleb – wolf
Tanner – wolf

Tammen Pride
~~Rhett – Alpha – lion~~
Trever – lion
Elijah (Eli) Reese – New Alpha - lion
~~Brent – lion~~

Luna – lioness – sister to Eli
Fancy Pants Shawnee – lioness
Amber – lioness
Petra – lioness
Brian – lion
Chuck – lion – owner of Dodson's Garage

Council Members

Alan Price – wolf - Nova's biological dad
~~Frank – wolf – Colton's dad~~

Remsen Pride
~~Jace – lion – Emory's former mate~~

Made in the USA
Monee, IL
11 May 2022

96238359R00114